Grieving Ground

ALSO BY JULIE BERGMAN

Los Angeles Fires of the Heart

The Finder, Poems of a Private Investigator

Custom Guitars, A Complete Guide to Contemporary Handcrafted Guitars (contributing author)

Grieving Ground

Julie Bergman

-Undercover Books-

Copyright © 2020 by Julie Bergman
All rights reserved. Published in the United States by Undercover Books

Library of Congress Control Number: 2020924122

ISBN (paperback) 978-0-9644458-3-3
ISBN (ebook) 978-0-9644458-7-1
ISBN (Kindle) 978-0-9644458-4-0

Extracts of verse from *Los Angeles Fires of the Heart* and *The Finder, Poems of a Private Investigator* by Julie Bergman are used with permission.

Manufactured in the United States of America
First Printing 2020

for my late sister, Carol

ACKNOWLEDGEMENTS

I would like to thank the many friends and colleagues who took the time to review this work and/or provide encouragement including: Walker Berwick, Phyllis Bagdadi, Therese Kosterman, Rosie Hanvey, Ian Lindsay, Lee Casey, Judy Reynolds, Florence and George Lowden, Karlie Burns, Kathleen Mauzy, Sheelagh Cullen, Sue Pelino, Sue Ennis, George Madaraz, Michele Haney, Terrance Burke, Robert Mason, Eric Bergman, Monty Curtis, Nancy Wilson, and proofreader Amy Brantley. I would also like to thank *Sisters in Crime* for their support of women writers. Lastly, thank you to Hart Hanson, Matt Goldman, and the inimitable Ian Rankin for the inspiration, and to Dick Francis and Sue Grafton, whose masterworks of the genre influenced me to write from the perspective of my career as a private detective.

Grieving Ground

Chapter One

There is dense mystery
in Edinburgh,
along the Royal Mile,
on the hills overlooking Holyrood,
North to the Firth of Forth,
in the North Sea air,
in the narrow closes,
the wet darkness of the past.
Tartan secrets,
disdained or celebrated
by the pint,
by the glass.
It always comes to me here.
Edinburgh, my spiritual zone,
danger and promise,
urban and ancient.
A pilgrimage,
urban and ancient.

Edinburgh felt damp. I welcomed that because
the day before when I'd arrived, it was an unusually

hot and dry June day. Very un-Scotland like. When Edinburgh isn't damp with rain, it doesn't feel or smell like a brewery by the sea. It doesn't feel like the magical town of my youth when I first came here from the States.

I was vaguely recalling mental images of my first trip here at age seventeen as though I were in a dream, when I realized it felt so damp because I was lying face down in wet grass in the middle of an old Edinburgh burial ground. As I put a hand under me to get up, there was a brief sensation in my ears of being underwater.

The pressure of a hand on my shoulder caused me to spin to my unsteady feet and step away, struggling to focus in the evening gloom on the person attached to the hand.

"I'm sorry to startle you. I saw you lying here and came over to see if you were alright," he said. "There was someone running away, heading down the steps when I came up. I didn't realize they'd left some harm in their wake. Sit down for a minute before you fall down."

At a loss of what else to do I complied, and the man who had materialized knelt beside me and was quiet.

Old Calton Burial Ground was up on a hill above Waverley Train Station. With a full moon rising, even though it was near to 11:00 PM, you could still make out the macabre idols pictured on burial markers from the 1700s and on. Standing tall against a backdrop of The Balmoral Hotel's clock tower and Waverley Train Station was none other than

Abraham Lincoln, watching over this lot as well. The statue was erected in the late-eighteen hundreds in memory of Scottish - American soldiers. The Scots knew about fighting for freedom. It was a reoccurring theme.

I'd come up the stairs to the iconic cemetery to see the moon rise over Arthur's Seat, the cliff edged hill that dominates the skyline of Edinburgh. It was one of my ritual things to do here, if the moon phases cooperated. I'd arrived in town earlier in the day ahead of a scheduled meeting the next morning with a prospective client named Aiden Lindsay. His cryptic communication to my Los Angeles private investigative business, where I'd gained a favorable reputation for finding missing people, was quite possibly equal parts fact and fiction. But he'd sent me a first-class ticket to meet with him, and he'd been referred to me by an attorney I'd worked with previously in Boston. The lure of Scotland tipped the kettle in his favor. He wanted my help finding someone, although he'd been vague about whom.

"Are you Mackenzie Brody?" he asked after a period of silence, waiting for me to gather my thoughts.

"Yes," I said, more confidently. "How do you know my name and who might you be?" The vertigo had abated, and I started taking stock of my condition. I had only been knocked down rather than struck hard; stunned but not rendered unconscious. I automatically checked the inside pocket of my jacket to see if I'd been robbed; my passport and mobile phone were still there. I was not carrying a bag, which would have been easy pickings, and perhaps what my assailant was looking for.

"You rather closely resemble a web photo of a certain private detective whose airfare and hotel I just paid."

"Ah, Mr. Lindsay," I said. "And what brought you here at this hour? Did you happen to be following me from my hotel?" Aiden Lindsay was becoming more discernable in the low light. He was obviously tall, looming over me even as he knelt. Compared to my five feet five inches he must have been six foot three. His hair was dark and thick with grey edges and he had a clean-shaven face and a forty-something, athletic body. He wore casual clothes and spoke with what sounded like a hybrid Scots - English accent.

"I was on the way to my pub just down the road and stopped in at your hotel to make sure you'd arrived okay. The concierge, who is a friend of mine, said you'd mentioned you were going to take a walk up here, so I thought I'd see if you were haunting the place."

"Yes, well I guess there's that. I wanted to see the full moon."

In any case, I expect you need medical attention," he said. "My car is just down Calton Road. I can take you to hospital."

Leery of this man in spite of his first-class invitation to Scotland to do an investigation for him, it hadn't escaped me that he was very possibly the perpetrator of my falling flat on my face. But I couldn't see a motive for him having done it. I was always looking for rational explanations. And I was quickly recovering my wits.

"I'm alright thanks. Just a minute and I will be on my feet."

"William Steele, date of death 11 March 1862. A newcomer of sorts to this hallowed hill," he said, leaning against a neighboring headstone and shining a light on the stone's engraving with his phone, waiting for me to gather myself.

I would not have known the face of Aiden Lindsay. I knew the author's name from bookstore browsing, airport stores, and the occasional espionage novel reviews. I hadn't read any of his work, being engaged in being a detective instead of reading about fictional ones. But given the slightly dubious circumstances of running into him in a graveyard at 11:00 PM after having just been mugged, it was entirely possible he was either strange, dangerous, or just lucky. I had no idea which.

"I'm sorry. This is not a crime ridden town," he said, turning off the flashlight on his phone. "I had no idea I was letting you in for an attempted robbery, booking you into The Balmoral down the street. Let's go down the hill to my local. Just a short walk when you're up to it."

I scraped myself off the ground and followed him down to Princes Street.

Chapter Two

I have these meetings
with people to ask questions.
I meet them in air-conditioned rooms,
or along satellite lines,
by video,
or on the tops of buildings,
in Spanish style bungalows,
standing on damp tile,
in dark theatres,
or on a bench by a river,
over bed,
over gun barrel.

I am always trying to find people. It's part of what I do as a licensed private investigator. I've almost always been one since the point when my young aspirations to be a spy were thwarted by no immediate access to an intelligence agency that I had any desire to spy for.

Working in the private sector gave me opportunities to travel for international clients to help in finding people, witnesses, or money. Canada, Ireland and the United Kingdom were all on the top on my list of desired destinations and burned into my Scots - Irish DNA and family tree.

As soon as I could break free from paternal oversight at age seventeen, I headed to the green isles that drew me like a magnet. Edinburgh was my first stop. I bunked down in bed and breakfast lodgings and spent months cloaked in the wet, winding, ancient closes and cobbled hilly streets. Grassmarket behind the castle was bohemian and a bit rough. The Edinburgh Festival every August was firing on all cylinders and the concurrent Fringe was a massive haven for artists of all types. The town smelled like the Firth of Forth near it and the pubs were always teeming and warm. It felt like home. As a teenage American girl, I was an attractive anomaly to young Scotsmen and I had many offers for dates, some of which I accepted. And I was once or twice in love.

I moved from Boston to Los Angeles in my early twenties but continued to travel to the UK and Ireland frequently, until the past few years when I'd been booked up with work in the States. Now back in Edinburgh, my usual feeling of being where I belonged was mixed with something unsettling. I wondered what was on my heels as I followed this Scotsman down the worn stone steps of the Old Calton Burial Ground.

I walked with Aiden Lindsay to Calton Road, one street, over to the copper and wood studded door of a pub. It was now closed for renovations, according to the sign, except for those who had a key to the Black Rose.

"I own this place with a partner," Aiden said, as we entered a dark room, past a flickering Belhaven Brewery sign. He touched a switch on the wall and lit up the bar area. "Usually, it's open until 2:00 AM. We've just closed for a fortnight to reconfigure the kitchen and the building contractors are halfway done with it. Have a seat. What can I pour you?"

I sat on a stool at the polished mahogany bar. "How about a Baileys on ice?" He gave me a wry glance and my client-author-bartender grabbed a bottle off the neatly organized shelf behind him and prepared a glass with ice.

"We should be reporting this assault in the graveyard, yes?" Aiden asked as he poured himself a pint.

"Not unless there were CCTV cameras there to shed some light, which I didn't see, or unless my assailant just poured me a Baileys. I'm perfectly fine. I just tripped over someone's grave."

"Albeit with someone's help. You landed on your face. Not so easy to do just stumbling over a grave." he added. I put a hand up to my face and wiped a piece of telltale dirt from my cheek. I didn't appreciate my client playing the detective.

"I wish I could have seen the person's face when I passed them on the steps, but whoever it was wore a motorcycle helmet."

"Well, I'm none the worse for it and still have my passport, so let's get to more immediate matters," I said, not wishing in any case to be taken anywhere by Aiden Lindsay.

Aiden leaned up against the bar. I noticed a wedding band on his left ring finger. He was fidgeting with it. "I would like you to find my mother, Alice Lindsay, who went missing two years ago on a trip to Boston. The police there had no luck finding any trace of her. She vanished. No credit cards used, no phone calls, nothing."

"What was your mother doing in Boston? I assume she was from this side of the pond?"

"She grew up in the Scottish Borders, although she went to school in England in Cumbria after her family moved down there. I was born in Cumbria after she married my father. He died years ago from heart disease. After that, we moved to Edinburgh to live with her sister, who has since passed away. My mother befriended an American professor from Massachusetts, who was doing a lecture at the University of Edinburgh. They met in the café at the Scottish National Museum. She followed him back to Cambridge, Mass not long after and was there for six months when she went missing."

"Was Alice with the professor until she disappeared?"

"Yes. His name is Thomas Costa. He claimed that she left him after a disagreement and returned to Edinburgh. At least that's what she supposedly told him was her plan, so he hadn't reported her disappearance immediately. My sister and I were the ones who filed the missing person report in Boston when we weren't able to contact her after that. The police confirmed she had not boarded a plane back to the UK."

Aiden proceeded to give me as much detail as he could recall and copies of the missing person reports. He explained that she had not at this point been declared deceased, as a declaration of presumed death from the Court of Session in Scotland can only be filed after a person has been missing for seven years.

As much as I originally suspected the man might have been the one to set me face down in the graveyard, his need for an investigator in the States appeared to be real. The bona fides he presented about his mother held up. And as usually happens when I am thrown a good problem to solve, especially with an open cheque, I was in.

"Why go looking for Alice again now?" I asked, curious what had set him off on this current mission.

"My wife, Cheryl, passed away eleven months ago of leukemia. I'm caring for our fourteen-year-old daughter. If my mother is still alive, she'd be just seventy, and it would be wonderful for Erin to have her grandmother in her life again. They were close. My wife's parents are both deceased."

"I'm sorry. It's a very cold disappearance, but I'll help if I can. You realize I'm based in Los Angeles, even though I am from Boston?"

"I saw from your website that you're licensed in both states, and one of my legal advisors whose firm has an office in Boston recommended you. You may have to spend some time in Massachusetts. I'll of course cover your expenses, Mackenzie."

"That works for me. I often travel to the East Coast and have colleagues who will help me out if I need more work done on the ground. And you can call me Mac," I added. "It's easier."

"Scottish surname, Brody, not to mention your given name. What's the link?"

"Scottish and Irish-Canadian grandparents on all sides."

"So, you're a good mixed drink."

"More like a Scots and Irish, Canadian-American blend with two passports."

I parted ways with Aiden after we made a plan to meet up the following morning to discuss payment arrangements for my expenses and fees. Instead of going back to The Balmoral, I walked up North Bridge and down Canongate heading toward the Palace of Holyrood. There were few pedestrians and fewer cars, being close to midnight. It had rained while we were in the pub and now cleared but the roads were shiny with moisture. Street sounds, as much as there were, were amplified against the old walls and newer edifices along the road. Edinburgh was a mix of ancient and modern, particularly in the Old Town where newer streets were built through or over some of the old closes. Sections of the Royal Mile in the Canongate had seen remodeling, but it still felt and looked ancient to me.

I walked toward the strikingly modern Scottish Parliament Building that was oddly juxtaposed against Arthur's Seat leaning ominously over the city in the distance. I noticed a car that was pulled over along the road. The engine was running, and someone was in the driver's seat. I crossed to the other side of the street to give it a wide berth, as shivers crept up my back. I had ghosts in Edinburgh in addition to my teenage larks. I pushed the thoughts aside as was my default response to unwelcome memories that were mixed in with the good ones, and started planning in my mind how I was going to find an impossibly missing person.

Chapter Three

Faces come to me, like so many
flashes of memory,
witnesses to some piece of history I
needed to investigate,
or a link to someone who was gone.
I've reached into their lives, drawn out,
pushed and prodded their memories,
finessed and protected their confidences.
Conflict and pain are often mingled with pride.
The Manhattan Project scientist,
the weapons builder, the chemical chef,
the cipher technician, the widower,
the teacher,
the warrior.
They all have a story to tell.

I'm always looking for someone. I might be looking for a man who worked at a company that spilled chemicals or trying to identify someone who is likely dead now but whose relatives can claim their long-lost relative's pension.

I don't do what investigators call 'domestic cases.' I won't investigate or conduct a surveillance on your spouse or ex-spouse for any reason. No one is ever happy with the outcome, not to mention that since your client is upset and experiencing financial stress, it's difficult to get paid. And even if the client swears on their mother's grave that they won't let their ex know that they've hired a PI, you can bet that they will manage to let it slip. Usually, to get back at their ex.

Given the above parameters, I love the process of looking for someone. People vanish without a trace sometimes. Our lives are all big to ourselves and yet when we go missing or die, the leftover memories and our heirs can be hard to find. Whether you died twenty years ago or forty years ago, I have to find out first who and where you were, in order to discover your people.

If you lived in an American city in the 1930s or '40s, you might be listed in the census records or the old city directories along with your spouse's name and employer. Wives usually didn't rate their own listing unless they had a job, and in that instance, they were mostly 'widows.' Otherwise, the wife's name was in parenthesis next the husband's name. If you had any African ancestry, you might have '(c)' next to your name in some directories denoting you as 'colored.' Some cities, early in the century, had a separate directory for the 'insane.' Which probably meant disabled. Heaven help us.

If you died in the 1970s or 1980s, your trail could be especially hard to trace. If you lived in a small town it was easier. The worst place to die was New York

City. It's nearly impossible to find people who lived and died in The Big Apple or even Long Island.

If you survived into the late 1990s, you started hitting the online paper trail, making my job easier. I would find your obituary in the local library or some record in the courts or find an old address and talk to your neighbors. In some cases, I might find the inscription on your gravestone and turn up relatives buried in the same cemetery. I would find your kids or your nieces or your cousins.

There were lots of ways you might have rated a mention in a local newspaper, which would also be helpful. Maybe you played in a successful sports league or had a wedding shower, and the resulting social pages article named all five siblings. Or depression might have led you to jump from a building in Chicago, or your brother might have fallen through the ice at age sixteen, or you didn't make it through a war, or you vanished in 9/11. I've seen it.

If you died in the last decade in the USA, it is fairly easy to find out who you were. The paper trail is fresh. Your obituary is probably on the web. My PI databases list you. Your past addresses and your property records are out there, perhaps along with your mug shot. Relatives bemoaned your loss publicly and the Social Security Administration made note of your departure.

If you were still living and didn't even know someone needed to find you, I would turn on the motor of my favorite search engines and drive down the information highway. But whether I could find a

Scottish woman who went missing several years earlier in Boston, where she was not a citizen, had no permanent address, who police detectives were unable to trace at the time of her disappearance, and whose body did not turn up, was an open question.

The morning after my late evening introduction to Aiden Lindsay, he called me on my cell and arranged to meet for breakfast at The Balmoral. He was ten minutes late as I waited for him at the entrance to the restaurant.

"Apologies for being behind schedule," he said, when he walked up. "Bit of traffic coming from the other side of town. They really should adjust the clock tower to ten minutes early rather than three, considering current traffic, then I'd have been precisely on time." The Balmoral clock looming over Waverley Station had been telling the slightly wrong time since 1902 when it was the North British Station Hotel, except for on Hogmanay when the year turned at midnight. The idea was to keep locals from missing their trains.

"I'm used to Los Angeles traffic. We'd need at least twenty minutes leeway on LA's Union Station clock. Possibly thirty," I said.

The waiter recognized Aiden and escorted us to a prime table and handed us menus.

"Do you mind being a known quantity around here?" I asked, as we were seated.

"I find it a bit awkward. Anonymity is my personal preference."

"Ask your publisher to stop putting your photo on book jackets?"

"Won't help for book tours. Or the social media presence required of authors these days. By the way, I noticed you've published a couple of books."

"Not best sellers. Worst sellers, actually. Poetry."

"Do you write about your investigations?"

"Only in code," I said. "That's what I like about poetry. Life and emotions in cipher. You don't have to outright admit to anything."

Aiden laughed. "I phoned up the local coppers this morning about your run in at the Old Calton graveyard last night," he said.

"And?"

"There was another attempted robbery down the street shortly thereafter, around midnight. Likely the same chap, went after a woman's bag while she was walking toward Waverley Station. He didn't get the goods this time either, as she screamed bloody murder and he got on his motorbike and took off. She got a good view of him before he donned the helmet, and the cops are on the lookout. Fairly young man, maybe late twenties. They think he's an out-of-towner. Not someone they've come across here before."

"Sounds like he had a bad night of it," I said.

"Better his bad night than yours. Apparently there have been a spate of these attacks in town every few months. Similar methods, so maybe the same lad. They'll catch up with him eventually."

Aiden handed me a piece of paper with his accountant's information. "Here's where to send the bills."

"Did you hire any private help when Alice went missing?"

"We did retain a Boston-based private investigator at the time, when the police weren't getting anywhere with it. The results were disappointing. Lack of results, I should say. Not even sure he did any interviews of people who knew her there. Thought I'd try again, and that maybe a woman detective might have better luck."

"We'll see how that goes. Sometimes it's an advantage. Sometimes not. But I'm nothing if not tenacious."

"I'm counting on that," Aiden said.

I had a flight to London from Edinburgh that afternoon, with one overnight followed by a flight home to LA.

Upon arrival in London, I took a share ride car from Heathrow into South Kensington and got there by late afternoon. I checked in at my usual, the Royal Garden Hotel adjacent to Kensington Gardens. The view from a garden-facing room was clear from Kensington Palace to the Thames. I headed out for a walk after depositing my luggage.

London was warm, bustling, lovely. The gardens were in full bloom. Dogs were playing in the park. Runners were crisscrossing the paths beyond Kensington Palace. Tourists and locals were strolling on Princess Diana's Memorial Walk. Swans were cleaning their feathers immune to the children

18

playing around the edge of the Round Pond. After circling the parks, I went at 7:00 PM to Côte Bistro on Kensington Court to meet a local investigator I'd known for years. I sat at an outside table along the cobbled side road off Kensington High Street and ordered a bottle of Sancerre. Five minutes later, Geoffrey Gordon walked up and sat opposite me, wearing a raincoat.

"Expecting some weather?"

"Always. Lovely that you're in town."

"I might be needing you," I said. The forty-five-year-old native Londoner had an investigative journalism background, and he was good at finding just about anything.

"Yes, thanks for the call. I love it when you need me. How have you been?"

"Well enough, busy. Running my shop in LA with just a couple of subs helping as needed. Traveling quite a bit on various cases."

"Still single?" Geoffrey asked. He was smiling. We both worked for the same international investigative company for a time; he in the London office while I was in LA. We dated on and off before I married, when I came over to London to visit or assist on cases. He was living at the time in a building in St. John's Wood, a stone's throw from the Abbey Road crosswalk, which was one of my favorite things about dinners at his place. I was as much a Beatles fan as the multitudes we'd see walking and or dancing and or streaking across Abbey Road.

"Still just once divorced," I said. "I'm too busy and I'm forty-something!"

19

"That doesn't mean life is over dear," he said.

"I am having a half-life crisis, and I'm not sure I want to share it with anyone."

He reached across the table and held my hand.

"You poor old sausage," he said.

"That's the nicest thing anyone has said to me. At least so far today."

Geoffrey was a sweet man, and a perennial bachelor and serial dater. I found out some years ago that I couldn't change that, and I wasn't sure I cared. I adored him anyway.

"How is LA? Are you still living on a yacht?" I'd been living in the marina on a boat since divorcing my ex a year earlier. He got the condo, and I got the 44-foot Tiara yacht with twin diesel engines that he purchased before we were married. Geoffrey liked to go sailing with his friends, and like most sailors, he considered power vessels to be the dark side of boating. Of course, he was right.

"I love my boat," I said. "I don't take it out much except to Catalina Island once in a while. It's mostly my floating home. It has a good amount of living space. But under power, she's fast, and beautiful. You should come and visit."

Geoffrey raised his wine glass. "When you get the sailing boat, I'll visit," he said.

"My next boat will have massive sails and a tiny diesel engine for when the wind fails to blow. Which is often, if you're trying to get to or from Avalon at Catalina, forty-four nautical miles out from Marina del Rey."

I laid out the facts for Geoffrey on the Lindsay case as far as I knew them. "Can you check out Aiden Lindsay and also look into Alice's background on this side of the ocean? I'd like to see what there is on Alice in the public record and also know more about my client."

"Any particular concerns?"

"The paperwork on his mother looks real, but I still don't entirely trust him. The incident in the graveyard for one thing. I don't know for sure if it was some other person who knocked me off my feet. And see if you can determine what he did after university, whether he has an intel background or something else. I need a better sense of this guy. I want to make sure he was leveling with me and that he doesn't have a hidden agenda. Or a record for domestic abuse or assault."

In the PI world, it's not unheard of to be asked to find a missing person for a client who has ulterior motives that they have not disclosed. Since you have to make sure that there is no secret or possibly nefarious purpose to the job you are being asked to do, it behooves the investigator to conduct some due diligence on a new client. Especially if they come via a referral that is a couple of steps removed. This was one of those cases.

"No problem," Geoffrey said.

After dinner and the bottle of wine we went back to my hotel together for the night. Geoffrey had to leave early in the morning for a meeting, so he was gone when I woke up. He left a spread of room service breakfast for me and a note thanking me for the evening. I wasn't sure if we decided to spend the night together for old time's sake, or just because we were both in the mood. But there's something to be said for spontaneity, and maybe the pleasant intimacy shored me up against what was to come.

Chapter Four

LA is a steady drone,
air and land,
by day, by night.
Freeways contingent on movement
soften but keep a grip at evening.
Hills seal in the air at dawn,
stopping, stultifying,
palms claimed by desert,
humans staled by enclosure,
glass and steel.
A life of white noise,
suspending, freezing,
blanketing pain,
voiding memory of green,
of silence.
There is respite only in the waves
that stroke the coast,
the salt ocean that commands
and cleanses.

I went to Heathrow at noon and caught my flight
to Los Angeles. Eleven hours and four movies later,
we touched down. The veil of haze over the dense

urban landscape was thick, and the hills brown. The contrast coming from the green islands is always a shock. Arriving in LA after a long flight also held some melancholy for me, since in past years I was usually met at the airport by my former husband, Peter Girard. It had been a year since we officially split, and I still ached every day. I missed living with him. I missed knowing he'd be there when I got home from traveling. Our marriage was destroyed by his eventual infidelity and I was glad I never took his last name.

I picked up my bag, cleared Customs, then took a shuttle to my car in LAX long-term parking. I drove fifteen minutes north to Marina del Rey, then pulled into the boater parking garage at my marina.

The marina was quiet, like it nearly always is in the evenings unless it's a weekend or holiday in the summer when more people come down to their boats. In recent years new apartments and hotels had been added to the county-owned parcels around the edges of the water, so it didn't feel like the cozy seaside harbor that it used to be. The influx of population from the growing tech companies in LA had made sure of that. But there was still peace to be had on the water, even on a boat sitting in its slip. I threw my bags on the salon couch, got a bottle out of the fridge and poured myself a glass of wine. I sat outside in the aft cockpit and shook off the travel fatigue, listening to the night sounds.

I'd grown up with small lake boats on the East Coast, and as soon as I'd moved to the West Coast, I started hanging around boaters and looking for opportunities to sail with friends, or motor to Catalina for the weekend. When I met Peter, he was retired from the Air Force and working as a commercial pilot. It's not uncommon for pilots to have a passion for navigating on the ocean as well. They're also very good at it, which was a plus as navigation skills were not my forte.

Peter was an intelligent, kind, handsome, single pilot with a beautiful boat. I wasn't entirely sure what he saw in me, not being overly confident in the relationship department, but by some miracle the feeling was mutual, and the relationship was a blast. It was all good until five years down the road when he began an affair with a younger paramour in another port, as pilots occasionally do, so I hear. I railed against the pain when he confessed. I almost wished he'd been better at lying, because I'd been blissfully ignorant. Missing the fact of his extramarital affair was pretty bad considering I was a detective. I put it down to being busy with work and not wanting to suspect the truth.

A light wind was rattling the mainsail halyards against masts on neighboring sailboats, and seagulls were calling out to each other overhead as they retired from an evening of fishing. The gentle motion of the boat had me nearly rocked to sleep. After a glass, I retired to the V berth in the bow, changed into sweats and a t-shirt and crashed into bed.

In the morning, I set my laptop up at the teak table in the salon and connected to the dock Wi-Fi. I dialed up my online databases and did some background searches on Hanford University

Professor Thomas Costa. In addition to pulling up his university bio, I looked for prior addresses, ran through the online civil and criminal court indices in Massachusetts as well as US District Court for federal cases and bankruptcies, and looked for property and relatives. The court indexes turned up empty, but they only went back so many years online. I would have my PI colleague in Boston search indexes manually at the court to look for archived cases.

Costa's online records showed both parents were deceased and although there were some other possible relatives listed, those were often inaccurate in the online databases and would need further scrutiny. I pulled his father's obituary off the web. The article said that his father, Thomas Sr., had been the owner of a popular nightclub in the Fenway Park area on Lansdown Street in Boston until he retired in the early 1960s.

I did not turn up any articles about Thomas or his missing friend Alice Lindsay in my historical news searches, but I hit on an article from the Boston Globe that referenced Costa Senior. There was no information in the article citing a link between Costa, Sr. and organized crime directly, but during a money laundering trial brought by the US Attorney's Office in Boston against a local faction of the Italian mob, Costa, Sr. was named as a co-defendant. The article also referenced that his nightclub had been shut down due to permit violations.

The rest of the day was spent doing laundry and re-packing my usual outfits of black jeans, blouses flats and sneakers, along with a dress just in case the need arose. A look in the mirror confirmed that my dark roots were beginning to show, but a visit to the salon to revitalize my light mid-length locks would have to wait. I had one client meeting on another potential case the next morning in downtown LA, then Boston was my next port of call for the Lindsay investigation. I booked a flight for the following evening and resigned myself to a continuing bout of jet lag.

Flying into Logan Airport in my old hometown was always a thrill. You can appreciate how the sea dominates this city as you're flying in over the harbor and the small islands that are visible along the flight path. Planes glide in low over the water and pick up the landing strip just beyond the shore. It looks like you are about to land in the water instead of on the runway, which always makes me sit up in my seat and hold my breath until we gracefully touch down on the tarmac.

I got my bags, took the shuttle to the rental car facility, picked up a rental and headed back to my usual base when I visit Boston. The apartment of my long-time friend, Morgan Kramer, was always at my disposal when I came through town. She lived fifteen minutes away from the airport on the edge of Charlestown. I often had her two-bedroom apartment on the second floor in the modern complex all to myself on my trips to Boston, as she traveled constantly working for a PR firm. She was in Chicago for a week this time, and I hoped she'd get back before I left town so we could catch up. Her place was convenient to the harbor and good restaurants in the North End. It was also close to Cambridge and a short walk to the Bunker Hill Monument. The 1800s-built granite obelisk on Boston's Freedom Trail had 294 steps to the top, which was my workout when I was in town.

After getting settled and taking stock of what she'd left in the fridge, I sat at the kitchen counter and answered some emails on my laptop. I looked over the list of possible threads to pull for Alice Lindsay's disappearance that I'd made on the flight. It wasn't long enough. I would have to improvise, and the visit to Professor Costa a few miles away in Cambridge would have to be done without calling him first, since he might not be amenable to an appointment. I planned to 'doorstep' him and hope for the best. It was one of my least favorite things to do as an investigator, because of how often the door does not open, or is summarily shut.

Professor of Economics Thomas Costa had graduated from Hanford College BA summa cum laude in 1969. He earned his PhD in Economics from Hanford U a few years later, and subsequently went to work teaching there. According to his university biography, he taught statistical methods to describe economic systems. He was a past Distinguished Fellow of the American Economics Organization, a past Fellow of the Econometric Fraternity, and had lectured internationally on his economic models. His online bio did not report the existence of a wife or children. He became a professor emeritus a few years ago but did not appear to have any ongoing association with Hanford or the economic forums, which I found odd in itself. As far as I was aware, tenured professors usually kept their hands in until death duly parted them from their university.

Costa lived just beyond the square in an enviable location on tree-heavy Francis Avenue. The street was lined with large classic New England clapboard houses. It was just a hundred yards as the crow flies from where Julia Child lived for many years and filmed several of her cooking shows. Her house was now privately owned, and she had donated her kitchen fixtures to the Smithsonian before she died. I wondered if they'd ever met, as according to property records, Costa had owned his home during the years she lived around the corner.

"May I have a word, Professor Costa," I said, when he answered the doorbell. I was standing on his wooden porch which was showing some wear and need of paint. "I am not a solicitor. I'm a private investigator and I've been retained by the son of Alice Lindsay to have another look at her disappearance." I spoke quickly, before he could shut the door.

Costa looked over eighty, although records showed he was seventy. His face was chalky white. The rest of him was portly and looked disheveled in baggy brown corduroy pants and a shirt that was half tucked in. Over the shirt, he wore the stereotypical academia outfit of a vest and braces; the latter fortunately keeping his pants up. He looked like he'd just woken up from a bender, with a couple days growth of beard and an unruly moustache with eyebrows to match. "Just a minute," he said, half under his breath. He left the door ajar but stepped back into the hallway behind him and reached for a pair of glasses from the side table.

Costa peered at me now from behind his glasses and under his overgrown eyebrows for a long minute without speaking. His grey-brown eyes were strangely magnified behind glasses that were perched at a slight angle on his nose, and the upturned ends of his shaggy eyebrows made it seem like he suffered from a perennial distrust. "Are you from the police?" he asked.

"No, I am a private investigator," I repeated, patiently. "I have been retained by Aiden Lindsay to look into his mother's disappearance."

It's not unusual to have to repeat two or three times just who you are and who you represent. People never seem to get it the first time. I am always forthright about my identity and who is paying my fee. If I approached an interview on a false pretext, anything I learned would not be admissible in court should there be litigation involved. And misrepresenting oneself as law enforcement would be a fast route to losing your PI license, not to mention your client and possibly your freedom.

Costa stepped out onto the porch and swung an arm to indicate that he was going to sit on an old rocking chair in the corner. He gestured for me to take an adjacent bench along the wall across from his creaking wooden throne. "I will answer a few questions, if I don't find them insulting," he said.

I sat down on the impossibly uncomfortable metal bench and leaned forward to hand him my investigator ID issued by the Massachusetts State Police. He looked at it and handed it back to me. "Alice was a long time ago now." He coughed without much containment, which made me nervous.

"Forgive me if I cover some of the same ground from when you spoke to the police back then. The notes that Aiden Lindsay shared with me from the missing person report were fairly brief."

"As I indicated to the police several times, I knew her for less than a year from the time we met in Edinburgh, and when she decided to move here six months later and stay with me. She was determined to come here even though I was not much in favor of it. She did nothing but complain for the next six months, until I asked her to leave."

"You asked her to move out?" I asked to clarify. The police report had quoted him saying that she had broken it off although he had wanted her to stay. "She was wasting her time and my time here." He practically spat out the word 'wasting.' And coughed again. Score one inconsistency.

"What did she complain about?" I asked.

"Everything. Did not like my kitchen. Did not like me going out at night with my colleagues. Didn't like my sister." Costa was raising his arms at each point as though he were conducting an orchestra.

His portrait of Alice did not sync with her son's view of Alice Lindsay's temperament. Aiden had described her as exceedingly kind with everyone and not prone to disagreement. But family members sometimes see a differing reality.

31

"Did she take an apartment here when she moved out?" I knew the report quoted him saying she flew back to Scotland immediately, but I was fishing. Looking for more inconsistencies.

"I paid for a plane ticket the day she left with her suitcases. That's the last I knew of her until a few weeks later when her son and daughter started calling here. Then the police said she didn't get on the plane." That information, at least, was consistent with police reports.

"What did you think happened?" I said, trying to engage him without putting him on the defensive.

"I've no idea and that's all I can tell you. Never heard from her again." Costa looked directly at me, and his diction had a sharp edge to it.

"Did she know anyone else in town here as far as you knew? Had she been introduced to any of your colleagues at Hanford or mentioned other friends in the States?"

"Alice went to a few dinners with some colleagues and I from the university. She never mentioned knowing anyone here. That is all I can tell you. That's all I've ever been able to say."

The aggravation in Costa's tone was building, and I was experiencing the sinking sensation in my stomach that an investigator gets when the interviewee starts to bail. Hoping to recover his attention, I tried a change of tack.

"Are you still lecturing at the university?"

"No."

That didn't work. Costa started to get up. I was losing him. He was heading for the door.

"Thanks for your time Professor Costa," I said, as he shuffled back into the house and didn't look back. The door slammed. I didn't get a chance to ask him if he had ever met Julia Child.

Chapter Five

Some things are consistent,
The voices that filled Cambridge
twenty years ago, fifty years ago.
Harvard's political players,
Berklee's reeds,
America's songwriters,
global minds.
They are all still live in the Square.
The mix of intellects,
races,
high purposes,
on display daily.

Cambridge hasn't changed much over my lifetime. Harvard Square continues to be the heart of it. Starting when I was sixteen and could borrow my father's car, I would come into the square with friends on weekends, driving in from the town where I'd grown up north of the city.

The Boston Tea Party was the best venue for the rock bands coming through town, but Passims on Church Street behind the Harvard Coop was the center of the folk scene; everything from Americana roots music to Celtic and in between.

There were great finds in the nooks and crannies of Cambridge; a restaurant on Brattle Street that served the best cream cheese omelets ever made, small shops with locally made clothes and jewelry, a used bookshop that was buried in the basement of the mock Flemish Harvard Lampoon building behind the square since the late 1950s. I would wind my way through the voluminous dusty stacks at the Starr Book Shop for hours, searching for gems. I went home with a lot of tomes on investigating and espionage. Useful research for a career in which there were no college degrees available, unless you went the criminal justice or forensic route. But however much I respect the skills and stamina of people who study morgue photos and flesh-eating bug timelines, it's not something I ever felt capable of doing. I don't even enjoy looking at blood spatter, which would seem to be a prerequisite.

I was on foot coming from Costa's house. I had ridden the T from Morgan's apartment to Harvard Square via the Orange Line to the Red Line, since it was always hard to park near the square. I walked back to Kirkland Street and made my way through Harvard Yard past the bronze statue of the university's namesake, out the Johnston Gate and down Mass Avenue.

I texted Jennifer Alden, my cousin's daughter, while I was walking. My cousins decamped to live in Florida, but Jen remained behind to do her master's program at the Hanford School of Government. She had already started digging around for me in the Hanford libraries since I'd emailed her before leaving London. I was looking for old university newsletters or publications that might have named some of Costa's contemporaries. She responded to meet her at the steps of the school.

Thirty minutes later I ran into Jen and we walked a block to the Charles River to sit down in the JFK Memorial Park. She was sporting new discrete nose piercings since I'd seen her the prior Christmas, and her silky black hair was three inches longer, nearly to the middle of her back. She wore a short black skirt, knee-high black boots, white blouse and scarf. Being one of my more fashionable relations since she'd hit her twenties, I was hoping some of her fashion finesse would rub off on me, but it hadn't happened yet. We sat on the concrete benches beside the fountain and spent a few minutes catching up on family matters. Then she pulled out a stack of papers from her backpack.

"You won't believe how many stacks of university newsletters I went through yesterday, Mac. They're not indexed, at least for the types of things you were looking for. I also went through a bunch of his lecture transcripts and some other documents I found in the economics department archives. I found several references to Costa and his departmental colleagues. I've made notes and a list of the profs and grad students who might have been associated with him."

"You are fantastic, you know. When are you going to quit mastering things and come to LA and run my office?"

Jen laughed. "Maybe soon, if I can stay on your boat."

"Done. Anytime," I said.

"I searched the faculty directories to see who on the list is still connected with the school. There are a couple people who might be around."

"This is so great. Thanks. Send me a bill. No good deed goes unpaid. I'll probably be here for another week or so. Might need some more research."

"I have projects due this week, but text me if you need anything else after that," she said. She handed me the stack of papers and turned to go back to the school, swinging her shiny hair and walking off with the confidence of a twenty-five-year-old with a plan to improve the world. I could only hope that she and her peers would succeed where my generation continued to fail.

My next day was spent tying up loose ends on another case remotely and researching online databases to find some phone numbers or addresses on the names Jen supplied. As was usual in this day of cell phones, it was not easy to turn up working numbers. Very few people kept land lines anymore.

I got lucky with Stephen Daniels. I reached him on his cell phone. He was a Hanford prof who had worked in the same department as Costa at about the same time period according to a newsletter Jen had found. Daniels said he would see me at an Irish pub at Faneuil Hall Market Place that evening. The fact that the pub where he wanted to meet was called The Black Rose, made me think the meeting was destined to be interesting. There were likely many Black Rose pubs besides Aiden's named after the Roisin Dubh, a Celtic legend about a black rose and also a famous 16th century Irish song. But I saw the coincidence of being in two Black Rose pubs in the space of a week as a good omen.

Faneuil Hall, the mid 1700s-built market and government meeting hall and the surrounding expanded marketplace was a thirty-minute walk from Morgan's across the North Washington Street bridge. The night temperature was cool for June and it was still light outside when I left Charlestown. I went into the pub and stood by the entrance until a man walked in fitting the description he'd given me. He introduced himself and we sat at a quiet end of the bar. I had already told Daniels on the phone about my interest in Alice Lindsay, and he said he would be happy to tell me what he knew.

Daniels was twenty years younger than Costa, and the years had treated him well. His brown skin was smooth, and with his close-cropped grey hair, blazer and dark jeans, he looked stunning in the dim light of the bar. Overdressed for a casual meet-up, maybe, but I couldn't help being impressed.

I ordered a glass of wine and Daniels ordered a pint. "How is Costa?" he said, "I haven't seen him in a long while."

"I only met him briefly. He seems well enough. Not especially forthcoming."

"That sounds right. He never was. More interested in the math of everything," Daniels said.

"Did you ever spend much time with him?"

"I ran into him off and on over a few years. I never got to know him particularly. He appeared to be going through a tough patch after his wife disappeared. He seemed kind of morose."

"Alice, you mean. I wasn't aware that they ever married."

"No, Sheila. This was before Alice."

I stared at my wine glass and collected my thoughts. Apparently, I hadn't done enough homework. A prior missing wife had not turned up in my preliminary research, Jen's research at the university, or the police reports on Alice. Another missing woman. "Can we back up? I hadn't heard about Sheila."

"I only met her a couple of times at university functions. She seemed to be a lovely woman. I remember her saying she was introduced to Costa through a mutual friend, and they dated for some part of a year before marrying. They were an odd match though. She was probably ten years younger and way more sociable than him. Costa struck me as an introvert."

"What do you remember about her disappearance?" I asked.

"Just what I heard around the campus. It was about a dozen years ago. Sheila didn't come home one afternoon after going to a store in Cambridge. Police couldn't find her or her body, so I guess that was the end of the story. I heard that she had one daughter who lived in Los Angeles."

"Two missing women," I said under my breath. "Did you hear whether he was a suspect in her disappearance?"

"No, I didn't hear anything like that."

"You said on the phone you met Alice Lindsay once. Can you tell me about that?"

"Alice was at a retirement dinner for one of our mutual colleagues a few years ago. I happened to sit next to her, so we talked. I remember that she was English or maybe Scottish. She said she'd just come to the States to be with Costa and was loving Cambridge, especially since she was staying a block from where Julia Child used to live. She was a big fan of Julia's. Thomas used to see Julia at the local market back in the day."

"Ah, I wondered," I said. Daniels looked at me quizzically. "Never mind. What else do you remember about her?"

"That's about it. When I heard that she had left, the word around campus was that she'd bailed on Costa and gone home. I wasn't aware that she was considered dead. I'm sorry to hear that he has suffered that pain twice."

"Yes, horrible and unusual," I added, thinking what investigators and cops often say about coincidences.

"One more thing. I don't like to spread tales about colleagues, but I heard it on pretty good authority that Costa ran into some trouble with the university, which is why he's not continuing to lecture there."

"Can you tell me what it was about?"

Professor Daniels hedged, looking at his watch. "Don't really want to go into details, without checking into it a bit more. How about I make a couple calls and see if I can get some info?"

"Yes, thanks, that would be helpful."

"I'll let you know."

I parted ways with Professor Daniels after some casual chat and returned to the apartment.

The first thing I did when I got back to Morgan's apartment was to sit in front of my laptop and do some online searches regarding Costa's first wife. In the archives of *The Boston Globe*, I found a couple of articles about Sheila Costa, nee Douglas. Thomas's name was not cited, which accounted for the articles not turning up in my prior searches. According to the write-up, she had gone missing after shopping at a boutique clothing store in Cambridge. Clerks at the store recalled seeing her, but after she left without purchasing anything, she was not seen again. Since she'd walked to the store from home, there was no car to trace and there wasn't much in the way of security cameras in that area then to capture her movements.

Thomas, just referenced in the article as 'the husband,' was said to have been interviewed by the Boston PD, but he was not determined to be a person of interest in her disappearance. Sheila Costa went into the bin of cold case adult missing persons. Police said that the husband's alibi held up; he was confirmed to be giving a lecture at Hanford that afternoon. The name of Sheila's only next of kin, her daughter by a prior husband, was referenced in the article.

I went looking for the daughter in my databases next. I turned up an old address in Massachusetts and a more recent address for Tammy Douglas in Malibu, just ten miles north of where I lived. There were six possible phone numbers. I dialed each of the numbers. All of them were disconnected. Working backwards from her address, I looked for and found several more possible numbers for residents at the same address who might be family members. As it was getting late, I put off making more calls until the following day.

Sleep was mostly elusive, as I was screwed up from the various time zones I'd been traversing. I eventually stumbled into the shower at six, then out for a walk around Bunker Hill by seven. It was too early in the day to attempt the stairs to the top of the monument. It wasn't open for another couple hours, so I took a walk around the neighboring hilly streets. The summer air was significantly less humid than it usually was during the spring in Boston and there was no rain in the forecast.

I was crossing the street in front of the apartment building at about eight, when a car turned onto the street from the adjacent parking lot and came racing toward me before I reached the sidewalk. I'd been glancing in that direction and caught sight of the car even before I heard the tires screech on the pavement. My first thought was that the driver was just momentarily out of control coming out of the lot. I leapt onto the sidewalk and behind a light pole for good measure, then turned to see the car swerve back down the road. I looked to see if I could make out the license plate, but the car turned onto the main drag and I lost a visual on it. A Black SUV of some type was all I could see.

"Effing Boston drivers." I said, to no one in particular, and pulled out the key fob to open the front door to Morgan's building. If I was still in a jet lag fog before, I was fully alert now.

Chapter Six

On the convoluted discovery trail
I'm distracted by the rock canyons,
the desert and the sea.
I get mixed up in needs and challenges,
waylaid by that which sparkles or chimes
in the search for others,
for proof of life.

Tammy Douglas had died so recently that it hadn't even shown up in my online databases yet, or in an online obituary in a quick search of news and social media. When I got through to her husband on one of the phone numbers listed at her address the next morning, he initially thought the call would be from the funeral home about the arrangements for her service. Carl Douglas, as he introduced himself, sounded understandably overwhelmed.

"She died last Friday." he said, followed by an audible sigh, when I asked to speak to Tammy. "She had breast cancer. Are you a friend?"

"I'm so sorry, I had no idea. I didn't know Tammy. I was calling to speak to her about her mother's disappearance. I'm a private investigator

44

based in LA, and I'm making some inquiries for a client about the Costa family history in Boston."

"I didn't know Tammy then. We got to know each other and married a couple years after her mother went missing. All I know is that she never turned up, never contacted Tammy, never used a credit card. Tammy thought she might have been killed in a mugging, or by Costa and her body disposed of, but the cops couldn't find any leads. She was eventually declared deceased so that her estate could be closed. Tammy was her heir in the will and life insurance, not the husband, so he wasn't suspected. No motive apparently. Sorry I can't help more."

"I apologize for calling at this difficult time," I said, hearing the stress in his voice.

"I didn't know Costa either. Tammy didn't talk to him at all after Sheila disappeared. He made no effort to stay in touch and never returned her calls. He didn't even know Tammy was sick. He couldn't care less, probably. I'm waiting for a phone call from the mortuary, if you don't mind, so I should go now. Call me in a few days if you want to talk more. Tammy's services are tomorrow," he said, and hung up. If he was curious about the reason for my looking into the Tammy's mother's disappearance, he didn't ask. He had more pressing things on his mind.

I had a call scheduled with Aiden Lindsay the following morning, and I was imagining myself telling him the only news I had was that there was one more missing woman, and one deceased stepdaughter in

45

the extended Costa circle. I expected a grilling from him. I got back on the computer, looking for some others on Jen's list of Costa's possible connections who might be able to draw back the curtain on the professor and his unlucky female partners.

The rest of my day was taken up with whatever catch up work I could do on the road. I touched base with a couple of law firm clients on pending cases on the West Coast and cleared my email to focus on Lindsay's investigation. His case was going to require some heavy background. My frequent partner in public records searches in Boston, a man who was not fazed by spending hours in dusty courthouse basements and state archives, was next on my list to pull in. I headed to Copley Square in the rental car to meet him.

Jimmy Burton was a retired cop turned PI whom I'd known for twenty years. I got to know Morgan through him since they had an on and off relationship, which was currently on. He quit before retirement age as a Boston cop after being grounded by a back injury while chasing down a rapist. His back problem took two surgeries to fix, but he settled into a new niche of doing some PI work on his own and conducting historical research for such as myself. He loved it, especially if it involved spending days at the library or government records centers, plus he still had connections on the force. That helped if we needed to do surveillance for an East Coast based investigation. Off duty or retired cops or feds were the best at surveillance. Personally, I didn't have the patience. Jimmy also enjoyed giving me unsolicited advice about my personal life, especially my penchant for living on the water.

I met him that afternoon in what was one of my favorite places to meet people; lobbies of major hotels where one is able to be fairly anonymous and sit in a quiet corner to talk without interruption. The Fairmont in Copley Plaza was close to the Boston Public Library, which would be the next stop for Jimmy after I briefed him on the case. A mega structure that dated back to the early 1900s, it reminded me of London's big five-star hotels, which is probably why I gravitated toward it.

"Is this where you are taking me to lunch after we talk, because I don't see any ocean here. Wouldn't you like to eat at Legal Seafoods and then visit The Constitution?" Jimmy said upon arrival. He was grinning wide. Jimmy was always smiling, which is probably why he had no trouble getting records clerks to do whatever he asked. His good looks and a slightly crooked smile that added to his appeal, didn't hurt either, I suspected.

I ignored the dig. "Let's stop in a café on Newbury Street for a bite after we go over the details." I filled him in on the case background and where I thought we needed to look to find out more about Professor Costa.

"The initial searches I ran online for Costa came up empty except for an article about his father's nightclub having been shut down by the authorities for some permit problems, and the old man having been named in a mob case in federal court. I'll forward that to your email along with the articles about the missing first wife."

"What else have you got in the courts?" he asked.

"No civil or criminal court cases showed up, state or federal, in online indexes for Thomas. I didn't see any other property records other than his Cambridge home, or names associated with him either, except his parents. I found his father's obit, but not his mother's. She died when he was seventeen and his father died about the time Costa graduated from the university. The father's obit said that the parents always lived in Boston. Thomas was the only son, and he has two sisters; Paula, who lived in Australia and apparently now in the UK, and Camila, who appears to be living just up the road. Thomas has virtually no presence on social media that I could find, unless it's buried on the dark web."

As Jimmy and I knew well, the online searches of court indexes only went so far back in years and often were incomplete. He would need to cover all the bases in the real world at the courts. "OK, I'll hit the court indexes, state and federal, check family law, bankruptcy, recorded docs, all the usual."

"Have a look for Sheila's and Alice's names as well in the courts, in case they turn up. If they were involved in any civil lawsuits, there might be names of associates they had here or people they had a disagreement with."

"We're lucky Costa is based locally and didn't live in six different jurisdictions," Jimmy said. "This won't be difficult unless he had a secret life someplace else."

48

"Don't discount that. Can you start with the old city directories in the library? I want to see where Costa was living back to when he left home for school, and cross check any addresses you find to look for roommates at the same address," I added. "Let's try to fill in the blanks on these people. Then if you could put in a public records request to get the police reports on Sheila's and Alice's disappearances, that would be good. I have the one from my client for Alice, but let's see if anything else turns up in the police files."

"What are you going to entertain yourself with while I'm doing all the important footwork and probably solving your case for you?" Jimmy asked. He chuckled in the rather charming way he does. I grinned back at him. The fake kind of grin.

"I have a client, a London investigator and a couple of professors to talk to," I said, checking my phone to make sure I hadn't missed any calls.

We headed off to lunch, crossing over Dartmouth Street to Newbury and scouting out a café. The stores were less locally owned than they were twenty years earlier, when I shared an apartment nearby with several roommates in an old brownstone that kept trying to burn down. It finally did after I'd moved out. I was a bit nostalgic for the small macrobiotic restaurants and basement pubs that had been replaced by fast food and shops selling generic goods. But the street still felt lively and full of promise, not in the least due to its proximity to Berklee College of Music and its rock student population.

After parting with Jimmy, I returned to the apartment before it got too late in the UK to call Geoffrey in London to see what he'd found out, and also make a call to Scotland to update my client. I parked the rental car in the outside lot at the building instead of the underground garage, since I planned to go out again later. As I stepped off the curb to cross the driveway, I had to stop suddenly in my tracks to avoid an oncoming car that came out of nowhere around the building and screeched around the corner to the main street, missing me by an inch. I cursed under my breath and this time got a better view of the rear of the vehicle – no license plate. Maybe the same black SUV with tinted windows. No view of the driver and in an area where there were no cameras. I was starting to feel like I had a target on my back.

Chapter Seven

This urban mass of lights
and darkness
engenders more fear than comfort.
Sparks that feed fires are ignited
with our human images held out,
playing the strong part.
But we're behind the flames
in embers,
ready to fall
into each other's arms
at the slightest passion.

When I reached Geoffrey, he said he had looked into the Lindsay family in the UK and hadn't come up with anything noteworthy. "Aiden looks to be on the level," he said. "No priors that I could find. No bad business deals that ended up in the courts. No murdered literary agents. An odd duck, by some accounts, but seems he's a talented and productive author. Ten best sellers in the last fifteen years. He keeps a low profile in town, but behind the scenes he supports a lot of charities. I had a conversation with someone in his long-time agent's office. He has a good rep with them, although he tends to drive them batty when he spars with his agent over publishing details. Same with his long-time editor. Hands on sort of guy," Geoffrey said.

"Any indication he has a background in intelligence? I wondered if that's how he slipped into writing spy novels. He might have been recruited out of university to do some work for one of the security services."

"There is a gap in his work history just after he graduated from Edinburgh University, but I couldn't find anything. And my rolodex of former British Security Service agents is non-existent. Ask him?"

"I will when I've gotten to know him better. Meanwhile I hope he doesn't try to micromanage this investigation. Anything interesting with Alice's background?"

"I found even less on her. Other than doing some secretarial work at a law firm in Cumbria while they lived there, and later at the University of Edinburgh for the dean's office, she didn't leave much of a footprint. She grew up in the Lake District on her father's sheep farm; one of two siblings. Her sister died last year, like Lindsay said. Alice didn't get remarried after her husband died. Just had the two kids. I wish I could have found you a smoking gun, but if there is a gun it's not smoking."

"That's actually a good thing, thanks. I am going to call Aiden next. I'll want to talk to his sister soon

also. I want her take on all this." After some more
banter, we rang off.

Aiden Lindsay didn't answer when I called him,
so I left a message and sent him an email saying only
that research was in progress, that I wanted to speak
with his sister, and to phone me when he had a
chance.

When the apartment doorbell rang, I assumed it
was a delivery service dropping off a package that
Morgan was expecting, since no one had called on the
intercom from the lobby. Checking through the peep
hole in the door, I didn't see anyone, so I figured a
package had been left by the door. I opened the door
and was blindsided by a large man wearing a black
neck gaiter pulled up over his mouth and a black
beanie covering his head, pushing me into the
apartment and forcing me back in a headlock, held
against his chest. I tried to scream but he had one
hand over my mouth. He dropped me to the floor in
the hallway, and I caught sight of his gloved fist
coming toward my face.

When I regained consciousness on the floor of
the apartment, my head pounded viciously. Sound
roared in my ears when I tried to sit up. From floor
level, I surveyed my surroundings and it looked like I
was alone. The apartment door was closed.

I felt my face and came away with some blood on
my hand, but my teeth seemed intact, and apparently
my nose as well. My cheek had taken the brunt of his
punch. Mentally thanking my assailant for avoiding
my important parts, I rolled over and did what every

modern person does after being attacked. I looked for my cell phone. I couldn't remember where I'd last seen it, but I hoped it was still in my possession and near my body, so I didn't have to go far to find it. Morgan had a landline, but it was many steps away in her den. Not to mention I didn't know anyone's phone number by heart, except 911, which I didn't want to call. I'm useless without the contacts information in my mobile phone.

The process of moving around was tedious, as I was not feeling quite capable yet of standing and walking. I slid my body as far as the living room couch and slowly sat up, leaning against it. I cursed myself for not having a smart watch. My old Tag Heuer could not be used to make a call, but it did indicate that I'd only been out for maybe fifteen minutes.

I sat still for a while, resting before attempting any further movement other than keeping the right sleeve of my blouse up against my left cheek. The pulsing sound in my head was diminishing, and the headache was not so overwhelming after a time. I finally noticed my cell phone on the edge of the side table and got to it without further complications.

I called the non-emergency Boston PD number first and asked for police assistance but said I didn't need an ambulance. Next I called Jimmy, who thankfully wasn't in the basement of the county archives where there was virtually no cell signal, so he picked up. "Come over to Morgan's place, like now, please?"

"Sure, be there in a few. I'm in the car now." That was like Jimmy. It didn't matter why I needed him, he'd be there momentarily, and he had a key.

Not even fifteen minutes later, Jimmy knocked then let himself in after yelling through the door that it was him. He beat the PD response team.

"Jesus Christ, Mac, what happened? Who did this?" he said, as he knelt down to my level where I was leaning on the couch and looked me over. "Did you call 911?"

"I called them, not the emergency number, before I called you. I knew you'd be faster anyways," I said. "How does my face look?" I pulled my sleeve away. Thankfully it didn't stick to my skin."

"Rough but no oozing. Few stitches might do it, or even none. Hopefully there's no fracture. Can you sit up on the couch?" He helped me off the floor, holding both my arms, and placed me gently on the couch.

"Doing better now," I said. I opened and closed my mouth. My jaw was working okay. "My head's clearing. It's going to be some shiner though. I have some good concealer. No one will know." Jimmy was unimpressed with my make-up regimen. He was busy looking around the room.

I gave him a quick rundown on my intruder. "No one I recognized. Big guy, probably over six feet, all in black. Happened so fast I couldn't even see his eyes."

"Doesn't look like the place was ransacked," he said.

"That's a blessing," I said. "Can you text Morgan and let her know what's happening, in case a neighbor rings her to say there was a ruckus?" Jimmy typed her a quick message to check in with him, and that all was okay.

"I've had a bullseye on my back since I started this case. Two anonymous attempts to either run me down or just scare me, and now a personal touch. Is my laptop still here? It should be in the den on the desk." He went into the den and yelled back that it was there. My bag was also still on the chair where I'd left it when I came in.

"So just a message, apparently," he said.

"You'd better watch your back too, Jimmy."

We looked up simultaneously when there was the sound of a siren outside. A few moments later there was a loud knock and announcement of police presence.

"I'm here and okay," I shouted, so it could be heard through the door. My friend got here before you, and he is going to open the door for you. I repeat, he is a FRIENDLY." Jimmy opened it, and two uniformed Boston PD officers stood there looking cautiously polite, guns holstered, and asked if they could enter.

Half an hour later, the PD took their leave after I'd run through the whole scenario with them. They declined bringing in someone to dust for some fingerprints, since I already reported the assailant was gloved. I told them about the near hit and runs, in case they were related. They were going to contact the building office to check if there was any CCTV footage and asked me what I was working on that might have brought the big man down on me.

I declined going into detail with the uniforms, begging off due to headache, so I was directed to call their detective division after getting patched up. Suffice it to say that PI work can occasionally go into overdrive. Like the time I had my life threatened on a case in Detroit, or when a witness to some illegal toxic dumping pulled a gun on me in New Hampshire. Or more insidious aftereffects, like when I came down with latent tuberculosis after interviewing a sick old truck driver, a witness on an environmental dumping case. He'd coughed all over me the whole interview. But based on his testimony we nailed the responsible parties for causing massive groundwater pollution, so I'd say six months of drug treatment to kick out the TB was probably worth it.

Jimmy drove me to the closest urgent care center, which was off Storrow Drive in Cambridge. As it was late by then, there wasn't much of a wait to be seen by a doctor. I didn't need stitches, but I was exhibiting some of the signs of a concussion and was advised to stay with someone and be woken up every few hours to make sure I could wake up. I tried to let that directive slide, but Jimmy insisted on staying overnight in Morgan's room, and he duly interrupted my repose several times in the night. I can't say as I was very polite about it.

In the morning he brewed the coffee and made sure I was able to function and eat before he left. I swore off all communication, silenced the phone after talking to Morgan at her hotel room in Chicago, and spent the entire day in the guest room bed sleeping on and off. Jimmy brought some dinner in later and made sure my symptoms were abating, and said he'd be back in the evening. Morgan had phoned him and directed him to stay with me at the apartment as my bodyguard.

The following day my condition showed improvement except for some lingering head and neck pain, the latter being whiplash from the frontal punch. I needed the concealer by now, as I had a bright purple shiner and a swollen cheek sporting what looked like road rash from falling off a bike. I decided that would be my public cover story, if needed. I'd talked over the case again with Jimmy before he left to do research in the morning, and we weren't any closer to figuring out why the attacks happened. The only possible angle I could figure was that Professor Costa had put some things in motion to discourage me from my investigation. His father possibly had mob connections, so maybe the son had friends in low places as well.

I asked Jimmy to pull the Racketeer Influenced and Corrupt Organizations lawsuit, otherwise referred to as a RICO case, which named Costa, Sr., to see what that was about. A follow up call with the PD didn't provide any help. There was no usable CCTV footage. The lobby camera wasn't working, and although the man could be seen on the elevator camera, his face was not visible as he put his back to the camera. I also placed a call to the detective bureau and was directed to leave a message.

As I was scrolling through some online research looking for another one of Costa's former colleagues to contact, Aiden Lindsay called back.

"How are things looking there, have you spoken with the Professor?" he said.

"Yes, and he wasn't helpful. He contradicted one point; he said he sent Alice packing when they weren't getting along. The cops had quoted him at the time saying she was the one who ended the relationship. Otherwise, he didn't deviate from the police report."

"What else? You mentioned a former wife?"

I spoke to one of Costa's former colleagues, who pointed out that some years prior to his relationship with Alice, Thomas Costa was married to a woman named Sheila who went missing. I talked briefly with her daughter's newly widowed husband, who said Sheila was never found and the prof wasn't a suspect. The daughter inherited her estate."

"Good Lord," Aiden said, taking a moment to digest the new information before he spoke again.

"I'll be speaking with the son-in-law again as soon as I get back to LA. He's in Malibu," I added. I briefed Lindsay on the research in progress, and then told him about my close calls and attack, and about Costa Senior's possible mob connections.

"I'm so sorry that this has put you in a hot seat. Is there any chance that the attacks could be a case of mistaken identity, that someone has confused you with the friend whose apartment you're staying in? Does she have enemies?"

"It's a reasonable question, but she works for a public relations firm that produces print and tv ads for innocuous retail products. And she doesn't have any skeletons; I've known her for years. And she's black and I'm white. Easy to tell us apart."

"Costa is looking even more like a suspect. I think we need to shut down this investigation. I won't put you in any more danger. I can find an ex-cop to do this."

"Whatever you think is best, Aiden, you're paying the bills. But I know and love several ex-cops and ex-feds who sometimes have trouble getting people to talk to them without flashing a badge. I'll head back to LA in a day or two, and meanwhile I have a roommate, so I'll be okay. My local investigator will continue the research on this end. I'll need to speak with you and your sister about your mother's friends who she might have talked or written to about her relationship with Costa. She must have told someone what was going on."

"Alright, why don't you plan to come back to Edinburgh next week. You can come with me to visit my sister, Sandra, in Cumbria. She has one of my mother's old address books and maybe some photos. We can look through those together."

"Sounds good."

"And be safe. Any prospect of further danger, we're done with this investigation."

After hanging up with Aiden, I reached another former Costa colleague by phone, a professor emeritus who worked in the economics department at the same time as Costa. We agreed to meet up that evening at the City Winery, which was ten minutes away from Charlestown by the Orange Line. I downed some ibuprofen to try and get through the interview and hopped on the train. I got off the T at North Station and walked down Canal Street and over to Beverly. I sat at the bar just inside the front glass doors. There was no concert that evening, so the restaurant was wide open. A burly Caucasian man sat down beside me.

"Donald Morelli," he said. He was seventy with a muscular build, close cropped dark hair, neatly pressed slacks and Oxford shirt, and tinted glasses that partially obscured his eyes. Something about him, which I couldn't quite place, put me on my guard. We ordered drinks and he ordered an appetizer. I deferred on ordering dinner. I was still feeling off and could not yet entertain the thought of food.

"Professor, thanks for meeting me. I hope I haven't taken you out of your way tonight. I appreciate your quick response as I'm not in town for much longer."

"What would you like to know about Costa and his lady friend from England?"

"What can you tell me about Alice? You mentioned on the phone that you never knew her but spoke to Thomas about her?"

Morelli took a long drink from his pint before he answered. "Thomas and I used to have a few beers occasionally when we were both working at the university. This was months after she went missing. He told me they met in Scotland and she grabbed his coattails to come to the States. Then she irritated the heck out of him for the better part of a year until he finally asked her to leave. She was a real bitch. Just wanted to spend his money and get him to marry her so she could get a Green Card. Sounded to me like she disappeared to make it look like Thomas offed her. A useless woman."

"What about Costa's wife, Sheila. Did you know him back when they were married?"

"We were both associate professors at the time. Knew he was married. Never was introduced to her. Thomas never talked about her and I didn't ask."

"I understand she went missing as well," I said.

"She probably couldn't get what she wanted from him," Morelli said, downing the last of his pint, and signaling the bartender for another.

Morelli went off for another fifteen minutes on a rant about how women thought tenured professors were a catch, and that men like himself and Costa had to watch their backs since women take advantage of them and their credentials. Morelli seemed to think that professors were the crème de la crème and that they were stalked by dissolute women on the lookout for doyens of any prominent university.

I was tiring quickly of his attitude, and since he seemed to have nothing concrete to offer and was exacerbating my headache, I made my exit as soon as I could politely do so. As I was walking back to catch the T, I was finding it hard to reconcile his description of Alice with what I knew of her so far. And although I sported swelling on my cheek and a shiner somewhat visible under the make-up, he never asked me about it. Being polite, perhaps, even if he wasn't kind in general about women.

When I got back to the apartment, I had a message from a Boston PD detective. I rang him back and spoke with Detective Blake Connor for the few minutes he could spare.

"I'm afraid we can't be of much help identifying who attacked you," Conner said on the phone. "Given the lack of evidence, unless further information turns up, such as what you might have done to instigate it. You might consider dropping your investigation of the missing Alice Lindsay and let cold cases lie."

"Yes, well thank you for your advice, Detective. I'm afraid I have a client and a job to do. But I'll make an effort to not instigate any further violence that requires a Boston Police response." I hung up with Connor and spent the next little while musing whether I'd been rude to the cop or justified in my response. I do endeavor to have a constructive relationship with law enforcement. I needed to try harder.

Professor Daniels texted me soon after I got off the phone with Detective Connor. He said he had some information for me about Costa's university troubles, and he wanted to speak in person. We agreed to meet along the Charles River on the Cambridge side.

I drove down Mass Avenue over the Harvard Bridge toward the MIT campus as the sun was starting to set. I parked just off Memorial Drive along the Charles and walked over to the Wood Sailing

Pavilion. I waited for Daniels along the pathway near the docks that were populated by various types of small sailboats organized into family groups. The lowering sun was reflecting off the Boston skyline, turning the buildings across the river into gold and reflecting off the glass spike of the John Hancock Tower. Intermittent raindrops were starting to fall, relieving the humid atmosphere. Professor Daniels took a place beside me at the rail. "I used to do some sailing here with my MIT buddies. I can't tell you how many times I flipped a Laser over and took a swim in the Charles. It's an exciting ride as long as you have at least fifteen knots of wind."

"Incredibly small boat," I said. "Give me a good forty feet at the waterline and I'm comfortable sailing." Daniels laughed. "Having said that, though, I used to take a sailing dingy out on the lake as a kid and intentionally flip it over, just to see if I could get it back upright."

"Never a dull moment on the water," Daniels said.

"And at Hanford, apparently. What else can you tell me about dear Professor Costa's tenure there?"

"He had a colleague in economics, Don Morelli. They did some grant research projects together. I didn't know Morelli – he's off the grid now like Costa, but I found out why the two of them aren't on board at the university now, at least in an active capacity. You piqued my curiosity about Costa, so I asked around."

"I know about Morelli. Some things at least, and they're not flattering. What did you find?"

"They worked on a government grant together and mislaid some of the funds about a dozen years ago. The university found out from a whistleblower in the department. It was dealt with internally and Costa and Morelli made restitution, but they were excluded from further grant projects. There was much less accountability back then. Now there are multiple layers of oversight. You can't spend a dollar without scrutiny."

"I can see that putting a damper on their involvement."

"And there was also a cloud around Morelli. He had a couple of sex harassment complaints from students. Nothing that was substantiated, but back in the day those claims weren't as vigorously investigated as they are now. Sad to say."

"Yes. Thanks for the information. It does explain why a couple of professors have taken on a low profile in their later years."

"Sorry about that black eye you're sporting, Ms. Brody. You didn't have that last time we met up. Your visit here has not been uneventful, apparently."

"Fell off a bike. I was hoping you wouldn't notice. Rain's washing off my makeup."

"Let's get out of the weather. Dinner?" Daniel's said.

"Sure, why not." We picked up our separate cars and met back over the bridge at an oyster bar off Boylston Street, across from the Hancock Tower. I was starting to like this guy. Maybe on my next time through he wouldn't be an interview for a missing person case. Good to get to know a tenured professor. Morelli would be disgusted with me.

After returning to Morgan's, I went online to book a return flight the next day to Los Angeles, then made a bullet point list of the research done so far and what was still to be done, with the end goal of finding out what happened to Alice Lindsay. The next phase would start with a plane ride back to Los Angeles and an interview in Malibu.

Chapter Eight

There is challenge in waking,
in breathing,
in seeing.
In walking onto empty beaches
and being still.
In being invited into the rooms
of others,
to see their pain.
In facing the calm
or the turbulence
with open eyes.

Pacific Coast Highway winds its way along the precipice of the North American continent at the edge of Los Angeles, spilling north into Malibu. Once you've passed the Santa Monica Pier and the popular beaches where Sunset Boulevard intersects the ocean, you come to a magical stretch of road that imitates Europe. There is an Italian spike in the landscape at the Getty Villa. Around the bend at Porto Marina you could just as well be driving along the Amalfi Coast, which the walls and stairways to the beach were built to emulate in the 1920s.

The morning after I flew back into LA, I was on my way to meet Carl Douglas, widower of Tammy, whom he had just buried a few days earlier. On my return home, I'd phoned Carl and he invited me to stop by their home on Big Rock Canyon Drive in Malibu to discuss the disappearance of Tammy's mother more than a decade ago in Boston. I hoped I would look somewhat presentable with a heavy layer of concealer on my face to cover the now yellowing hue of my bruised cheek and black eye. The head and neck aches were abating but the color was still cycling through the spectrum.

Big Rock was uphill from PCH, not far beyond the intersection where Topanga Canyon Boulevard meets the sea. The contemporary ranch house was perched on an acre of land overlooking the coast. When Carl opened the door and invited me in, I walked into an airy living room that was open to the kitchen, with a view of the choppy Pacific below from nearly every window. Three short, white fluffy dogs enthusiastically grouped around my feet as soon as I sat on the couch.

"Don't mind the dogs," Carl said, shooing them in the direction of dog beds in the corner. "They are pests, but I don't know what I would do without them. This house is suddenly very empty. Can I get you anything to drink?"

"No, I'm good, thanks very much." I was reaching in the direction of the dogs to pat them, when they shuffled off to their beds. I had dog deprivation, not being able to own one now since I traveled so much. My last dog, a loving and opinionated English Springer Spaniel, who Peter and I shared until she died at thirteen, wouldn't have been nearly so obedient.

"I'm so sorry about Tammy. Had she been ill for quite some time?"

"She beat down a tumor four years ago, but the cancer came back with a vengeance in the last ten months. She was in and out of the hospital, but when all her options for treatment were exhausted, she decided to stay at home and see it out here. I'm glad she was able to be with me in the end. The hospice people were wonderful and made it as easy as it could be."

"Do you have any kids?"

"Two sons and one daughter by my first wife. All off on school and careers now, but they've been on deck for her and for me. One of our sons is going to move back in with me next week as soon as he packs up his apartment in the Palisades."

"What do you remember about Tammy's mom? You said you didn't meet Tammy until after her mother disappeared, but did she talk much about her?"

Carl kicked off his shoes, propped his feet up on the ottoman in front of him and cleared his throat. "Sorry, I'm hoarse from all the talking with family these past few days. Tammy loved her mom, but said they got along better at a distance. They hadn't lived close to each other since Tammy went off to college. Family home was outside Boston. Lexington, I think.

69

Her mom was a principal at the local high school where Tammy attended through 12th grade. You can imagine how that went. Not well. Tammy was an only kid and got a lot of oversight. She thinks her mom invented helicopter parenting."

"How did Tammy end up on the West Coast?"

"Came out here to go to UCLA and put down roots. Sheila and Tammy's father divorced and then he moved to Ohio or somewhere and dropped out of the family. Sheila met the professor at some point after that. I think Sheila and Costa were married only about a year when she went missing."

"What do you remember Tammy saying about her disappearance?"

"Just that the cops were on it and couldn't come up with a trace of her. As I said on the phone, Tammy was the sole heir on Sheila's will and life insurance, so Costa had nothing to gain by her eventually being declared dead. In fact, he didn't even pursue it. Tammy did all that. She was the executor of the estate. Tammy only met Costa once and didn't like him. They never talked much after the disappearance, and she didn't stay in touch with him afterwards. I think she blamed him, even though the cops didn't."

"Did Tammy ever mention her mother saying how the marriage was going with Costa, whether there were any problems?"

"There was the occasional phone call between Tammy and her mom, but of course it wasn't like now where everyone is constantly emailing and texting. I know they exchanged some letters. Tammy kept at least some of Sheila's correspondence. If you want to borrow the letters, I know where she kept them."

"That would be great, if you don't mind. I'll mail them back to you right away. Maybe they'll shed some light."

Carl went into another room, followed by the three small floor dusters, then came back a few minutes later with a folder containing a stack of letters.

"I hope these can be of some use. Feel free to make copies. Tammy always hoped that her mom would turn up, or at least that the police would find her body, so she could have some closure."

I thanked Carl and was about to make my exit when he called me back.

"I just thought of someone else you might want to talk to. Before I married Tammy, she was dating a guy named Frank Kelter for a couple of years and it was during that time period when her mother was with Costa. I remember her saying they went together to visit Sheila in Cambridge at the time. I don't know if he'd know anything. I reached out to Frank last week to tell him that Tammy had died. I'll send you his phone number."

"Thanks, I appreciate it." I headed to the car and took off down the hill and south on PCH to the boat. Traffic was fairly light since it was overcast and cool for an early summer's day. Not good beach weather, but a perfect quiet time to sit on the boat with a cup of tea, soft country blues tunes coming from the speakers, and review Sheila Costa's letters.

The sun was setting, and lights were going on around the marina when I got back. I unzipped the canvas covering over the boat's aft deck and ducked inside to unlock the cabin door. Other than the occasional sound of an airplane coming in for landing at LAX a few miles away, the marina was quiet. I was the only live-aboard on my dock, since the county only allowed a limited number per marina. Unless it was a weekend, I hardly saw the owners of the neighboring mix of power and sailing vessels.

Sheila Costa's handwritten tomes to her daughter were lovely. They were several pages each, written in a flowing cursive. The writing expressed a lot of affection. I found myself embarrassed to be looking into the private relationship between mother and daughter.

Most of the dozen letters described Sheila's days walking around Cambridge or shopping and meeting friends for lunch; she didn't seem to have been working. She described the weather in detail, a preoccupation which I always associated with the Brits, not Americans. She also wrote about her anguish in being separated from her only child, although she wrote that she could understand the attraction of California and why Tammy had chosen to go to college there. There was one mention of Tammy visiting Cambridge to see her mom.

Passing references were made in the letters to her new husband, Thomas Costa, and the home they shared in Cambridge. Sheila expressed a contentment at having found another relationship. The letters were all written in the one-year timespan after she married

72

Costa and until she went missing, which made sense as that was the period when Tammy had left home to attend UCLA.

Several of the letters described events Sheila attended at the university with Costa, mostly dinners and lectures at the faculty club. I had sorted the letters chronologically from earliest to last before delving into them, and the final couple of letters had a slightly different tone. There was less casual description of her days and the letters were shorter in length. There were two mentions of a colleague of Thomas's whom she found, in her words, 'distasteful,' Donald Morelli. Sheila met him at faculty club dinners, where she described him as 'barging in' on her conversations with others and being obviously inebriated and disrespectful. I found that interesting, considering Morelli told me he'd never been introduced to her.

I put the letters aside when I felt a headache creeping in again and went down into the cabin to prepare some dinner on the galley stove. Since I'd been on the road, there wasn't much food on the boat, but I rummaged up some rice and veg, just enjoying the fact of being back in the marina. One part of me was quite happy to be a rolling stone without much in the way of roots or commitments, and the other part liked a home and routine. The two sections of me were always quietly tugging at each other, producing a chronic malcontent. I lived with the mercurial warp and woof of my being as best I could.

My boat's berth was at the end of the dock, with her bow facing west. In a smaller berth opposite mine, I kept a twenty-foot Chris-Craft Speedster that I'd bought myself. The runabout was too small to take over to the islands, but unlike the big boat I lived on, which I didn't take out without additional crew, I often got in the Speedster and cruised around the marina by myself or with friends. She had a beautiful blue hull with a red racing stripe, teak decking and trim, and was immaculate in spite of being fifteen years old. On a calm evening I liked to take her out past the harbor jetty and open her up. She'd cruise an easy 35 MPH and topped out at 50 MPH with her 225 horsepower Mercruiser inboard motor. I liked speed. After having dinner, I thought about taking her out, even though it had already been a long day. The Speedster won out anyway. I pulled off her cover, warmed up the engine, threw the lines off onto the dock and backed out.

The sun was just going down as I flicked on my navigation lights and settled into the helm seat at the wheel, cruising slowly out to the main channel toward the jetty and open sea. Sea lions on the docks at the park across the channel were barking, and a few pelicans were patrolling for a late supper. I passed one of the Hornblower's vintage yachts, the Zumbrota, carrying summer night revelers. Once in the main channel past the Coast Guard station, I kicked her up to 8 knots in the channel between the north and south jetties, staying to starboard out of the buoy-marked sail zone. Rounding the bend to go north past Venice Beach, the ocean was a still lake. Perfect sea conditions for a runabout that was more suited to small bodies of water. I ran north parallel to the beach as far as Venice Pier, then circled to port and back toward the marina, cruising at about 20 knots. The exhilaration of being on the water, in whatever type of vessel, never got stale. With mental cobwebs erased by the wind and salt air, I took her back home.

The next day, I got a text from Carl Douglas with the contact information for Tammy's old boyfriend Frank Kelter. I called and reached him right away.

"I'm close by the marina, in Venice," he said, after I explained why I wanted to talk to him. "I can meet you at the pier later, if you want. I'll tell you whatever I can remember about that Cambridge visit."

I walked down Washington Boulevard at 2:00 PM to look for Kelter at the entrance to the Venice Pier. There were plenty of people around on the long concrete pier; locals walking their dogs, tourists, a busker with a battery-operated guitar amplifier. A few fishermen were swinging lines over the sides into the water further down the pier from where the waves were breaking amid a handful of surfers.

I didn't recognize Kelter from the description he gave me of a sandy haired, tan, older white guy in shorts, t-shirt, and sunglasses There were many of those. But one of the men fitting that picture stopped me, having recognized my description, and introduced himself as Kelter. There apparently weren't as many women my approximate age and height wearing a baseball cap that said 'Caerleon.' It was the name of my boat. She was named after a town in Wales with a legendary fortress, thought by some historians to have been King Arthur's Camelot.

"Shall we take a walk?" I said, motioning toward the Pacific Ocean end of the pier.

"Yeah, sure. What can I tell you about Tammy? I was so sad to hear she had passed. I didn't even know that she was sick. I'm glad Carl called me."

"As I mentioned on the phone, I'm interested in anything you might remember about Thomas Costa. Carl said you visited him in Cambridge with Tammy at some point."

"I met Tammy when she moved out here to go to UCLA. I went back East with her once, when she wanted to visit her mother. It was kind of weird."

"How so?"

"We met Tammy's mom on her own a couple times for dinner, but the one time we went to the house when we were supposed to have dinner there with Sheila and her husband, Costa wasn't there. Instead, his sister was there. Can't remember her name. She said she was sitting in for him because he had a lecture to give at the university."

"How did that go?"

"The sister was a piece of work. Condescending to Sheila and Tammy. Made us all uncomfortable. That was obviously her intent."

"I guess there was no love lost between Tammy and Thomas Costa, from what Carl told me."

"Tammy figured he'd skipped the dinner on purpose and brought in a proxy, who was less than welcoming on purpose. She didn't make any more attempts to get friendly with him after that. Not while

I was dating her. She didn't know what her mother saw in him. But it's that way with a lot of kids and a parent's second spouse, I guess."

"Did Tammy ever mention a colleague of Costa's named Donald Morelli? Or did you happen to meet him on that visit?"

"Name doesn't ring a bell. Don't think I heard his name mentioned. We didn't see anyone on that visit other than Sheila and Costa's sister."

Kelter and I turned around after getting to the circular end of the pier and walked back. Gulls were lined up on the railing, waiting for some wayward pieces of bait or a discarded catch from those who were fishing. A couple of snowy egrets that were perched on the rail eyed us warily as we approached and took off as we walked closer. A couple of guys on skateboards narrowly avoided running into us. A typical Southern California summer day.

"Were you still seeing Tammy when her mother went missing?"

"No. We'd broken it off a few months before. But she called to tell me. We were on pretty good terms. What do you think happened to Tammy's mom?" Kelter asked.

"No idea at this point. It's a really cold case, but thanks for the info."

"One other thing that sticks in my mind about that visit. The sister, she prepared the dinner. It was pasta. She said she couldn't eat it for some reason I don't remember, so she ate something else. Tammy and I and her mother all got sick afterward. We were up all night at the hotel. Tammy figured we'd been poisoned."

"Misfortune seems to follow those who follow the Costas," I said.

"Well, good luck with whatever you're doing," Kelter said, as we parted at the street end of the pier.

I walked back to the marina up a crowded Washington Boulevard, past the Cow's End coffee shop and the murky end of the Venice Canals. As I opened the gate to my dock, I saw the silhouette of a familiar figure standing by my boat, in the uniform of an airline pilot.

"Peter, what brings you?" I said to my ex, not altogether excited to see him. He didn't usually stop by unannounced and I preferred it that way.

"I was just in the hood. Boat's looking good. Get her waxed recently?" He ran his hand over the side of the hull.

"Yeah, few weeks ago."

"You're looking good too, Mac. Except for the shiner."

"Nice of you to say." I thought the residual yellow under my eye was invisible. I didn't bother to explain.

"I'm heading to the airport. Flight to Denver. Wondered if you'd like to have dinner when I get back."

"Maybe not, Peter. I can't go there. Not right now."

He bent down and tidied up the end of the dock line, which didn't need it. "Alright then. Talk soon," he said, and walked up the dock.

Maybe after a year of separation he was starting to realize what he'd lost. I didn't care. The betrayal was still too fresh, and I was in no mood for a repeat performance.

After a couple more days of recuperation, during which time I made copies of Sheila's letters and posted the originals back to Carl Douglas, I headed to LAX for the overnight ride to the UK. Once I'd checked into the airline lounge to wait for my flight, I caught up on some calls. I phoned Jimmy to see how the Boston research was going and to add to his list of things to do. He was still in the middle of court searches, which I expected because the archived civil records took days to request through the court clerks. He had, however, finished the criminal searches in state court.

"Mac, you might not be surprised what I found on Professor Costa so far. He was working nights in the office at his father's club while he was going to university. One of the club's waitresses got a restraining order against him for threatening her with bodily harm. The woman also claimed that she was threatened with being fired for refusing the advances of the club owner's son, but I couldn't find any lawsuits relating to it, so it didn't go any further."

"Huh. How did it go with the old city directories?"

"I found listings for the family residence. Just the parents, Thomas and two sisters. No other tenants named. Looks like he lived with his parents in Boston until going to school. Then I found one entry for him living at an apartment in Cambridge, which listed his occupation as student. I cross checked the address and found one other student name listed at the same address in the same year; Don Morelli."

"That name keeps coming up. He is the prof who I met with the other day, and who got into trouble along with Costa with a grant funding scam. And he had sex harassment claims. He lied to me about having met Sheila Douglas Costa. I read some of her letters to her daughter while she was married to Costa, and she clearly remembered meeting him and his obnoxious behavior at a couple of university club dinners. He didn't mention having lived with Costa while they were students either; he said they met for beers after Costa had been married to Sheila. We need to look into him further and deeply."

"On it," Jimmy said.

"How about the racketeering case?"

"Can't get access to the files – the case was sealed, but I did look at the docket and got the names of the other co-defendants. Costa Senior was dropped as a co-defendant early on. Also, I got a response on Alice's missing person report. It is a duplicate of the one Lindsay gave you, so that was the complete document, and there was no additional paperwork. My request for Sheila's report is still pending. They weren't computerized in Massachusetts until the 1990s, so it's an archived paper trail."

"Can you send me the names of the other defendants in the RICO case? Maybe one of them would be worth interviewing."

"I've already run through the names and came up with one guy who is still alive and in the area. His name was Charles Pickering. I'll email you his address. He's 85 now. Looks like he went down to the federal farm for a few years as a result of the case."

"Good, I'll look him up to see what he knows about the Costa family."

"Alright. Be careful with that one. He's a convicted felon. Maybe or maybe not reformed. I'll join you for the interview."

"I'll let you know," I said.

"I should have the rest of the court searches wrapped up this week. Morgan is back from her Chicago trip. She was sorry to miss you and appalled that you were attacked in her apartment. She hopes you'll want to stay there again."

"I'll email her from the plane. I'll be back in Boston soon. Just let anyone try to mess with me when Morgan is home. Remember when she foiled a burglary at her old apartment? Sent the intruder screaming out the door when she went after him with kitchen knives in both hands."

"Yes, I try not to upset her," Jimmy said.

Chapter Nine

The smell of ale and whisky wafts through Edinburgh
 like breath
from the breweries and distilleries
 on the port side of town
and the remnants of past spillage on
cobblestone streets,
transported year after hundred year
to the horse cart's rhythmic beats
or the syncopated rattle of four wheels
or the muted streams of townspeople
leaving the pubs at closing,
last pour in hand.

The aroma of cooked grains is mixed
with the sharp perfume of the North Sea,
and captured in the salt-fermented tree woods
that brace the city's human-made structures
with their arms.

As ripe as Guinness and more ancient
than the Scot's high walled castle,
the city is washed and fermented
by waves of liquid time.

Aiden picked me up at Edinburgh airport after the one-hour flight from London's Heathrow. I'd slept a couple of hours on the overnight flight, so I wasn't the extreme bundle of jet lag that I usually am on arrival in the UK. I could deal with another few waking hours before sleep. International jet setting was tiring, but I relished it. He greeted me outside the terminal, and we walked to the carpark and his car. There was a light rain putting a sheen on the cars.

"Welcome back. How were the flights?"

"Better than usual – no delays," I said, as we exited the airport.

"We can go to my flat to have dinner, if you'd like, then I'll drop you at The Balmoral."

Since the research Geoffrey had done on Aiden hadn't shown any red flags, and the information Aiden had given me to date had held up, I was no longer apprehensive about him, even if I still had some questions about his background. I accepted his invitation. "Sounds good," I replied. The rest of the drive was spent in small talk, as I didn't want to discuss the investigation until the following day, when I'd had some sleep.

We pulled into a narrow drive twenty minutes later that led to his apartment complex in the West Coates area of Edinburgh, just beyond Haymarket. The building itself was modern and low key, but it sat on the property of the palace-like former home of the Donaldson School for the Deaf. The Donaldson had been converted into flats, but the outside of the historic sandstone building was untouched except for cosmetic repairs. Appearing every bit of a late 1800s home for royals, the former Victorian hospital complex sported corner towers with angular turrets, elaborate stonework and a central tower, all surrounded by acres of lush green park. The orphan hospital, built with a bequest from publisher Sir Jimmy Donaldson, was opened by Queen Victoria in 1850.

Aiden's flat in the recently built adjacent complex was a two-bedroom penthouse on the third floor overlooking the Donaldson from massive windows in the living area. When we arrived, his housekeeper was just leaving, having put out a dinner spread for us consisting of a hot vegetable and pasta dish topped with smoked Scottish salmon. Aiden invited me to sit at the large glass dining table, and he went to the fridge to get a bottle of wine.

"Erin is visiting a friend. I hope you'll meet her next time," Aiden said, of his daughter, as he sat opposite me at the table. "I did some of my own research the other day," he started, as he poured us each a glass. "I found an old article in a Boston paper about the tragedy with your brother when you were young. Seems that would be enough to put anyone on a career path to finding missing people."

"I guess you could say that. I always wanted to be a detective though, from the time I was very little. My mom and dad called me the finder. I was always looking for things. It didn't matter what it was. We lived on a lake when I was small, and my mother lost her diamond engagement ring in the water off our boat dock. I spent months looking for it in the shallows by the dock. Just after she passed from lung cancer, I found it. I was thirteen."

"And it must have been the following year that your brother went missing?"

"Yes," I said.

"I'm sorry. Perhaps I shouldn't have brought that up about your brother. I'm sure it must be a difficult subject."

"It isn't something I talk about very often."

"Please, don't if you're uncomfortable."

"I don't know how much the papers reported, but it was a carjacking. I was in the passenger seat, my dad was driving and my nine-year-old brother, Kenneth, was in the back seat. We were stopped at a light on the way to visit friends south of Boston, and a man stuck a gun in my father's open window and ordered him out of the car or he would kill us all. My dad hopped over the console and pushed me out the passenger door. Before he could pull my brother out of the back seat, the guy had gotten behind the wheel and sped off. We never knew what happened to Kenneth. Two weeks later, the car was found down in a gully with no bodies in it, but some of Kenneth's blood."

"Those weeks must have been agony, followed by a lot of unending grief," Aiden said.

"It nearly destroyed my father. He was drinking a lot after that, and so depressed he could barely function. He wouldn't let anyone console him or offer him support. He'd lost my mother to disease only the year before. Then his only son. It was very, very sad."

"I can't even begin to imagine," Aiden said. "How long did your father survive?"

"He is still alive. I've done the best I can to be there for him, but it's been difficult. Has dementia coming on now. He's in a memory care home north of Boston and he's in good hands."

"Do you ever get to see him?"

"I talk to him occasionally but haven't seen him for several years. He hasn't wanted to see me. He tells his caregivers he has no family. I call and check on him with the staff there regularly. Trying to visit him just got to be too much."

"Were there no leads as to who the carjacker was or what happened to your brother?"

"No fingerprints in the vehicle. My father, as well as one witness who saw the car speeding off, gave descriptions to the police and there were composite drawings done. We looked at endless mug shot photos at the police station, and my father was called in to look at a few dead young Johnny Does as well, which was utterly horrible."

"That's bloody awful," Aiden said.

"There was a mug shot of one man that my father thought looked like the perp, but when the cops checked him out, he supposedly had a solid alibi for that day. He was out fishing off the coast with two other men who vouched for him, and he produced a photo of himself holding up a catch which he said was taken that day. Not even a scrap of information ever turned up about Kenneth, not from unidentified bodies anywhere in the country, or in response to broad publication of his photo. All the usual efforts."

"I saw some of the articles with the wee lad's photo. Did you take the search further when you became a PI?"

"Of course. Even before I got licensed. I've revisited it off and on over the years, looking at any possible angle, including doing my own background investigation and surveillance on the guy my father thought he recognized. A man named Stone Hadley. He'd been arrested before for assault and battery, although not convicted because the charges were dropped."

"Did you turn up anything new on the Hadley guy?"

"Not much of anything. I interviewed the two men who he went fishing with on the day and they stuck to their story. The photo the guy offered to back up his alibi was suspect as it was obviously taken in clear weather, but it was cloudy all over the basin that day. The detective in charge of the investigation got so tired of me he refused to take my calls, but they did work the case well and long. It's hard to believe Kenneth's abduction was over twenty-five years ago. I still have dreams about him."

"I expect that never goes away, especially with no end in your situation. I dream every few nights about my wife, and it has been nearly a year since she died."

"How long were you married, if you don't mind my asking?"

"Eighteen years. We met at university. She was from London and came up to Edinburgh to get her teaching degree. We waited a few years to have the kid. She was always healthy until the last couple of years when she started having persistent fatigue and was losing weight. She was diagnosed with an aggressive leukemia, and it worsened quickly. Her mother passed away from the same disease, so it was likely to be genetic."

"I'm sorry, Aiden."

"She wasn't willing to go the whole chemotherapy route, when she was told it would be unlikely to prolong her life for more than a short while. She wanted to have some quality of life before dying. We had a few months at the end where the three of us stayed very close and had some memorable times being together non-stop, just cooking meals, watching films and having laughs. Cheryl could find the humor or irony in just about everything, including her own illness."

After dinner, Aiden and I sat downstairs in the living room with the curtains wide open, looking out on the lights of the Donaldson on the finally clear evening. We had minimal discussion about Alice Lindsay, as I was struggling to stay awake and we would have a couple hours the next morning to talk about it on the drive to visit his sister. I shook off the sleepiness long enough for Aiden to drop me off at my hotel, and I barely got my clothes off before I sank into the bed.

The drive to Penrith in Cumbria the next day took just over two hours. Aiden picked me up at The Balmoral after I had breakfast, and we headed south. We took the A702 south to the A74 and hit very little traffic. Penrith was on the northeast edge of England's Lake District. The drive took us through smooth green hills and pastures populated with sheep. I filled Aiden in on the details of my research as we drove, and where I thought the investigation should go from there; the priority being to learn more about Professor Costa's relationship with Alice, and for however it might relate, the fate of Costa's first wife. True to form, Aiden grilled me on all the details.

"I'm to understand that you don't like coincidences?" Aiden asked. "I've written enough spy procedurals, if you can call them that, to think it sounds hackneyed. I don't even allow my protagonists to say that."

"I don't like no bodies! Think about it, Aiden. How many people have one partner go missing, let alone two? There has to be a limit to bad luck, although I'll grant that the circumstances could have been different from one to the next. One or both partners could have committed suicide somewhere where they weren't found, or they could have been abducted and killed by an unrelated assailant. No bodies are the problem," I said.

"My mother could be alive," he reminded me. "With no bodies, anything is still possible."

"We'll try to get you some closure, one way or the other. Did you start writing spy novels before or after she went missing?"

"After. Before that, I was writing biographies of historical literary figures."

"Do you have a background in intelligence? I wondered since it's sometimes the ex-spooks who start writing espionage novels."

"I went from university to a bit of traveling and writing. Don't know a lot of spooks. I've studied a lot. Enough to fictionalize the life." It didn't get past me that he hadn't actually answered my question. I decided to leave it there. I'd find out eventually.

"I guess we're both trying to solve something," he added.

Sandra Cotter, Aiden's sister, lived in a sprawling brick country house with her husband about ten minutes from central Penrith. A herd of sheep, some with red splotches of paint on their backs, showing they'd recently been serviced and by which ram, scattered in front of our car as we pulled down the long dirt driveway.

Sandra met us at the door and ushered us inside after shaking my hand and giving her brother a kiss on the cheek. She was two years younger than Aiden with the same tall, thin build and petite features. Her husband was at work at a local manufacturing plant and their three twenty-something aged kids were distributed around the country. She was working from home designing websites for retail clients. Afternoon tea and biscuits were already set out on the large oak kitchen table.

"Please, sit down and have some refreshments. I've pulled out Mum's old address book and some photos that we can have a look at together," Sandra said.

Alice's address book was a six-inch by eight-inch spiral bound folio. I leafed through it briefly and saw that the entries were all in pencil, neatly written out on their properly alphabetized pages. No email addresses, just street addresses and presumably landlines.

"I think she had transferred whatever names she needed into a newer book before she moved to the States. I found this old one in with her papers," Sandra said.

"Did you contact any of the people listed in there after she went missing, to let them know and ask if they'd heard from her?" I asked.

"My husband, Henry, and I went through it at the time and called the names that we recognized as close friends or work associates. You'll see some are marked with a red tick – those were my notations of people I reached. If there's an X next to the name we tried the phone number, but it was disconnected, or just plain no answer after repeated attempts."

"I remember going over those with you and Henry at the time," Aiden said. "There was no one who had any significant news of her since she'd gone to the States."

"What do you remember about when she met Professor Costa, and how it led to her moving to New England to live with him?"

"Henry and I were living here and raising our children. I went up to Edinburgh about once every six months, and she came here to see us maybe three times a year. The first time she mentioned him, she said she'd met a man who lectured at the university. They got along well, and she was hoping to keep seeing him. I think he was around for a few weeks, because he was going to a seminar in Glasgow too, or something. Aiden, you probably know more about that since you saw Mum more often."

Aiden added, "I wish I could say I had more insight about that time, but I was busy meeting book deadlines. Mum was living in Marchmont, while I was over on the other side of Edinburgh, and the twain met only occasionally. We did talk on the phone once a week. She told me about meeting the Professor and that he was the first man she'd had some interest in since our father died. I was rather stunned when she announced a few months later that she was moving to Boston at least for six months. But I thought it good she was coming out of her self-imposed shell."

"Did either of you see her just before she moved?" I asked.

"We had a small going away party at her flat in Edinburgh. Henry couldn't come, but I drove up with the kids on a Sunday. It was also my birthday, so it was a combination event," Sandra said. "Aiden, you were there if I remember right."

"I came by for a bit. We were all asking about the Professor. She had just known him for the few weeks he was here, but she said they spoke on the phone frequently and she decided to give it a go in Cambridge. She was taken by his intellect more than anything, I think. She said there was no discussion about marriage, that he was more of a good friend. Though from what I remember her saying, she hoped the relationship with him would progress to more."

"None of you had met him?" I asked.

"No, that was a bone of contention with Sandra and I," Aiden said. "But Mum said she would give it six months, the duration of her visa, and spend the time checking out New England. She rented out her flat in the meantime. She was pretty good about staying in touch. She had a laptop and mobile of course. She sounded good and as if she was enjoying it, though didn't say much about Costa. We gave all those emails to the Boston Police when they were investigating. They never found her suitcases or her laptop or her cell phone. There was no indication of problems with him or anyone else in the calls we had or in the emails we received."

"You might try contacting this woman," Sandra said, leafing through the address book to the letter S, and pointing to the name of Mia Strom. The name had a red check beside it. "She was Mum's closest friend, at least from the time she lived up north. I don't know if Mia has moved again, but she had relocated from Edinburgh down to Galashiels in the Borders the I last spoke to her. When I called her after the disappearance, she said that she had received a few calls and letters before that, but no mention of trouble. She hadn't heard from our mother for about a month before she went missing."

"That's great, thanks. Anyone else special who comes to mind? Colleagues, maybe?" I asked.

"Aiden?" Sandra said, looking at her brother. "Any ideas?"

"I actually didn't know any of her work colleagues. The dean at the University of Edinburgh who she worked for at that time was an old man. Last I heard he was gone."

Before leaving, we looked over some family photos. Wedding pictures showed the couple on the steps of a registry office with just a few friends to witness - typical post war. She had a short bob hairstyle and a very present look in her eyes. Later images of her with her grandchildren showed her having aged gracefully, with the same bright eyes and soft features. There was one undated picture of her in a garden, sitting on a bench with her best friend, Mia Strom. Mia was going to be my next call.

The drive back to Scotland was spent in part listening to Aiden describe his passion for literature. He was a voracious reader of a wide swath of literary genres; everything from mysteries and sci fi to classics. He immersed himself in the written word, reading and writing.

"How did you come to own half of the Black Rose? Seems contrary to your other endeavors." I asked.

"Owning a local is a good way to stay in touch with humanity, when much of your day is spent in a book world," he said. "But truth is, I only bought in on it right after my wife died. It was either that or give in to my propensity to shut down social contact after Cheryl left us. Erin was the one who encouraged it. Couldn't stand me moping about. She was the one who insisted we have another look for my mother as well. I have a lot to thank her for."

Aiden kept both of his leather gloved hands on the wheel of the Jag as he spoke and took the tight bends in the road like someone who had found his purpose again.

94

We pulled into Edinburgh around dinnertime and parked on George Street across from the Helly Hansen store. We backtracked on foot to St. Andrew Square, and went to have dinner at The Ivy. After salads and salmon, we walked back along Rose Street and stopped at an Italian wine bar for after-dinner drinks. The local nightlife in Edinburgh was in full swing, with pub patrons spilling out into the warm air and gathering in boisterous lots; not the least among them being groups of Frenchmen and women in town for a Scotland-France rugby match. In spite of Aiden's self-described awkwardness at being recognized in public, he was graceful to the few who acknowledged a well-known local author in their midst.

Aiden dropped me off at my hotel late in the evening, and since I was adjusting somewhat to the time change, I slept through and woke up to my cell phone alarm at eight. As arranged, I headed over to Aiden's apartment, walking the two miles from my hotel. The morning was clear and cool. Rush hour traffic, such as it was compared to LA, motored along while I walked along the Princes Street Gardens. Tourists streamed out of the train station and buses, stopping to observe a sole busker as he played Highland pipes for an early morning audience across from Waverley station.

I took a detour up Lothian Road past St. Cuthbert's 19th century church and west through the Haymarket, which was less like I remembered it from past visits, as it was undergoing various construction projects. Time wasn't standing still, even or maybe especially in Edinburgh.

Aiden buzzed me into his complex and met me at his door. He offered me coffee before we started on some phone calls.

"Mac, this is Erin," Aiden said, when his daughter came up the steps from the lower floor of the apartment. She looked more like seventeen than her fourteen years and had the tall and slender build of her father, but with a lighter complexion and hair. Where I'd been maybe expecting the perennial teenage summer outfit of a short skirt and sandals, she was wearing tight jeans with multiple holes and Doc Martens. She came over and shook my outstretched hand.

"Just getting something from the kitchen. Nice to meet you," she said, then quickly disappeared back downstairs to her room.

Aiden and I settled down to make calls. Mia Strom was first up. Her phone number listed in Alice's handwriting was picked up by a message machine that confirmed it was still her number. Rather than leave a message, I put her number aside to call back. I randomly dialed a few more of Alice's friends who had red ticks beside their names in her address book. Although they'd been reached initially by Aiden's sister just after her mother's disappearance, I encountered a bunch of disconnects. That was no surprise considering the likelihood that most of the landlines had since been replaced by mobile phones.

Mia Strom answered on the first ring the next time I dialed her number. I introduced myself and said I was with Alice's son, and helping him look into his mother's disappearance once again, in case we could turn up some new information.

"I can't talk to you," Mia said cautiously.

"Aiden is here, and I will put him on the call if that would reassure you," I said. Before she could respond, I hit the speaker phone button and Aiden called out a greeting from across the table. "Mia, if you know anything that could help us about Alice's relationship with Thomas Costa or what happened, please let us know. So far we've not located anyone she mentioned anything to about him while she was in Boston."

"Hello Aiden," she said, speaking quietly. "I'm sorry. I wish you well," she added, and hung up the phone.

"That was odd," Aiden said, echoing my thoughts.

I'd barely put the handset of Aiden's landline down when my cell phone rang with the caller ID showing it was Jimmy in Boston.

"Mac," he said. "I'm glad you picked up. I got the Boston PD records on their investigation after Sheila Costa went missing. Your Mr. Morelli was the subject of a police complaint on him by Sheila two weeks before she disappeared, then she retracted it a week later. She alleged that he was stalking her. Morelli was initially a person of interest due to that, but they couldn't find anything to involve him in spite of his friction with Sheila. Professor Costa was cleared, like

Carl Douglas said, since they couldn't find a motive, let alone a body. Costa also vouched for Morelli as well as giving him an alibi and was quoted as saying Sheila had a misunderstanding with Morelli and realized she'd overreacted."

"What's with these two professors and their female relationships?" I asked. "Alright, it's time to have another talk with Morelli. I'll stop back in Boston on the way home to LA. Please tell Morgan I'll be coming."

Aiden and I decided we would drive down to Mia Strom's home the following day. She lived just an hour drive south on the A7 in the Scottish Borders. Her reticence on the phone was strange, and we didn't know if she was in ill health, or for some other reason was backed off from speaking with us. In any case, I hoped that seeing Aiden in person would allay her fears.

The remainder of the afternoon was spent dialing more numbers from Alice's phone book, searching for updated numbers for those we couldn't reach, and speaking with a few old friends who had nothing interesting to offer.

The picture of Alice that continued to emerge, both from speaking more to Aiden about her and discussions with several of her old friends, was that she was kind to a fault, intelligent, well read, and truly compassionate with others. If anything, she was overly permissive as a mother, and spoiled her children rotten. Which might account for her son thinking that I was his personal PI.

"You'll just do this case, right?" He said, as we paged through the phone book. "I wouldn't want you to be distracted."

"I do have a life and other jobs, Aiden."

"This case is pressing."

"Summer is a slow time for the attorneys I usually work with. They go on vacation. You don't own me though, that would cost considerably more."

"How can I keep you focused on this, Mac? We have a lot to do." Aiden looked up from the phone book, giving me his 'direct' look. I was getting used to that.

"Flying me between continents in first class helps. No guarantees though."

"I'm used to writing about government employed spies. Privates are a universe unto themselves."

"You're right about that. Lots of different backgrounds. We're ex cops, feds, spooks, journalists, housewives. An eclectic freewheeling bunch."

"Heaven help me," he said.

"Just do the best you can, Aiden. It's not so complicated. Just give me some room."

The rain was blowing sideways when we stopped for dinner in Edinburgh. Aiden parked near North Bridge, and we went down the Scotsman Steps which link the Old and New Town. A few hundred yards further up Market Street, we went into The Doric, which was one of my favorite restaurants going back years. Aiden shook the rain off the umbrella we shared. We went upstairs past the fiddler and guitar player who were working through some trad tunes by the bar. We sat at a small table in the far corner in the upstairs dining room with a view of the street below, which was at least partially obstructed by scaffolding. Edinburgh – always under construction.

After we picked out a bottle of wine, Aiden ordered their massive plate of fish and chips, while I went for the vegetable gratin.

"You're single, yes?" Aiden asked, as we waited for our meals.

"Yes, divorced a year ago."

"No kids?"

"Not even one," I said.

"How goes it with your ex, if you don't mind my asking?"

"Haven't seen much of him since then. It's not that we're not civil to each other when the occasion arises to cross paths. There's history there. On both sides. On mine, I guess it was the promise of a long relationship shattered. On his, maybe he feels bad for messing it up. Or not."

"I hope he feels bad," Aiden said.

"You're not going to write about this investigation after we finish, are you?" I asked, wanting to change the subject.

"Too personal. My life is not the life of my protagonists. And my daughter wouldn't appreciate it," he said, smiling. "She was barely a teenager when my mother left for Massachusetts. They got along famously."

"How is she coping since your wife passed?"

"I suppose like any teenager, there are things going on in that brain that I'm not privy to. But we've always been close, and she seems to have some supportive friends her age. I think she's okay. Her schoolwork was suffering for a time, but she got back on track before the summer break."

"She's about the same age that I was when I lost my mother, "I said.

"That hadn't escaped me," Aiden said. His brown eyes were looking intently at me. This time, I had to look away.

"Sorry, I didn't mean to go there," I said.

"You don't have to apologize, Mac. You're my partner in this. The clan and my sordid past come along with the package."

"I have yet to hear about your sordid past. I can't wait!"

After dinner, instead of heading right back to the car, we turned up towards the High Street and the dark hulk that was Edinburgh Castle. As it was late and the rain was still blowing in spurts, there were no tourists, just the occasional car and a few locals on their way to somewhere.

When we approached a black Mercedes that was pulled over with the engine running, I stopped short.

"Let's cross the street?"

"Sure, no problem," Aiden replied. We crossed over the slick road to the opposite sidewalk. As we passed it, the car pulled out onto the street and drove off.

We stopped in the Esplanade and looked over the wall toward the university where Alice Lindsay had worked in the dean's office pushing papers.

"What was with the car back there?" Aiden asked.

"Sorry. Visceral reaction I have when I see a vehicle parked like that with the engine going."

"Kick off a memory?" Aiden asked.

"You could say that. The first time I came here, a man who was sitting in a parked car in the Old Town with the engine running got out when I was walking by and grabbed my arm. He tried to pull me into the back seat. I got away from him, but the flash-back to when my brother was carjacked was intense."

"That must have been frightening."

"While he held my arm, I told him in no uncertain terms that I was leaving, and he let go. Shocked at my response, I think. I wasn't scared until I was walking away. I didn't run and didn't look back to see if he was following. My heart was pounding in my throat and I nearly choked on the déjà vu."

"This is a town with a lot of ghosts. Sorry you've run into a few of them."

"Every time I think I've gotten past that fear, I get hit sideways again."

"Does that only happen to you here?"

"In Boston and Cambridge as well. I tend to cross the street a lot. Those cities have some of the same darkness as your medieval towns. But some of the same excitement. They're artistic and academic hot beds like Edinburgh," I said. "I could imagine that Alice would have felt at home there."

"Yes. We have to find out if she died there."

Chapter Ten

I have yesterdays that keep disappearing
further behind,
and present moments searing inside
for release.
I'm holding on for balance
and hiding my weakness from
those who might see.

Intensity colors this undertaking
with risks I cannot perceive.
The rain sounds like clapping and laughter,
The future is a danger surrounding me.

The next morning's weather started off dark. Rain clouds were roaring in overhead, and drops were coming down in fat batches. Aiden met me with umbrella deployed, and I got in his car for the ride to the Borders. We headed toward Galashiels, an old mill town adjacent to the undulating green pastures that characterize the Borders, interspersed with the winding ninety-seven-mile course of the River Tweed.

By the time we reached Mia Strom's house, the rain had let up, though the cloud cover remained. Her residence was in a row of attached brick terrace homes, probably constructed during the 1960s or '70s, with a view of a golf course. We parked along the back side of the buildings that faced the street and went to the rear door. Aiden rang the doorbell and we waited.

After several minutes, a young man peeked through the curtains on the door window, then pulled open the door. He was probably late twenties, though his substantial weight and unshaven face might have made him look older; definitely not Mia's husband, if she currently had one.

"What's up?" he said, looking startled, though it wasn't apparent why. Perhaps we'd woken him up.

"I'm Aiden Lindsay. Are you Mia's son? You wouldn't remember me, but my mother, Alice, was close with Mia. I think I met you when you were about ten."

"Aye, I'm Danny. I know who you are. My ma's no' here."

"Sorry to stop by unannounced. This is my friend, Mackenzie Brody," he said, nodding to me. "She's helping me run down some old friends of my mothers' to see if we can turn up anything new about when she disappeared. We called Mia yesterday, but she seemed reticent to talk, and I thought if I came by in person…"

Danny shook an unkempt head of dark hair. His drooping jeans and sweat-stained checkered shirt barely contained the already bulging shape of his twenty-something body.

"She left last night. Said she was going to visit a friend and she hasn't returned yet. I don't know where she is. She takes off sometimes for a couple of days at a time. I know she has a boyfriend and doesn't want me to know," Danny said. "I've seen her getting picked up in a car by a man. She could just tell me. She divorced my father a lot of years ago. I'm no bairn. I don't fucking care," he said.

Aiden pulled a business card out of his wallet and handed it to Danny. "Could you please ask her to ring me when she's back."

Danny took the card, said nothing and closed the door.

Aiden and I finished up the evening back at the Black Rose on Calton Road, as he wanted to check the progress of the renovations. After he looked in on the construction in the kitchen, he poured me a Baileys without asking and sat beside me at the bar.

"Back to where we started, Mac," he said, with his energy seeming to leak out of him.

"We're not done yet. We've shed more light on Costa. We've got another suspect in Morelli, at least with Sheila's disappearance, which could be related. Not to mention that someone was after my hide in Boston. It has to be connected to this case – it has been months since I was there doing any other work. There would be no reason for that attack unless there is more to know."

"Is it so unrealistic to think that my mother could still be with us? Maybe I'm deluding myself and you.

And overwhelmed with raising a daughter on my own."

"I wouldn't have agreed to help you if I thought there was zero chance. We've got no body, so as you said, there is a chance your mother is still alive, somewhere. At least we should find out what happened to her."

"My mother was never depressed – suicidal, as far as I know. I don't think there is any chance that she killed herself. There is someone who caused this to happen, whether she was murdered or could have been injured and lost her memory of who she was. She ran into the wrong person. Maybe most humans have that capacity for evil."

"I hope that it's not 'most' people. I think the majority of people just want a productive life and to take care of their families. There's only a small percentage of humans who would kill you for no particular reason or just to take what you have."

"Okay so it's not the many. I hope she didn't run into the few."

As Aiden dropped me at my hotel, we made plans to touch base the following day after I landed in Boston. I planned to take a taxi in the morning to the airport for my flight from Edinburgh to Boston, changing in Dublin, since he had promised Erin to drive her in the morning to Fife to see her cousin.

I was saying my goodbye in the car when he reached for my arm and held it. "You'll come back here soon, Mac, even if you don't find out anything more in Boston?" There was anticipation in his voice, but his brown eyes weren't giving any more away. For a moment, my voice was caught in my throat.

"Yes, absolutely I will," I said.

The seven-hour flight to Boston via Dublin was easy. Anything less than the eleven-hour flight from UK to LA felt like a breeze to me. As we landed at Logan Airport, the rain was coming down in sheets, as though welcoming me back from Scotland.

Jimmy met me at the airport, and we drove to Morgan's apartment in Charleston with the wiper blades on full tilt. We had a reunion dinner, with Morgan now back from her work trip.

"You'll be kept in good health here, Mac," Morgan said, as I settled in. "We'll see to that. Jimmy is going to stay over the whole time, packing his 9 mil., and we've installed our own security camera in the hallway and made sure the lobby camera is now fixed."

"I'm not worried. I'm not sure the heat is warranted, but I'll leave that up to you, Jimmy."

Over a post meal glass of wine, Morgan and I caught up with each other, then I sat down with Jimmy and went over the progress of the records searches, and any loose ends we could still pull.

"I want to visit Charles Pickering tomorrow, and I want to go see Morelli after that. I will refresh his memory about rooming with Costa in university and knowing Sheila Costa as well and see what he has to say. And hope he'll want to deflect concerns about his bending the truth and his university hijinks to spill some details about Costa. Nothing loosens the tongue like self-preservation."

"Good luck with the two of them. Let's hope you can get some straight answers," Jimmy said. "I'll drive you up to see Pickering in the morning and watch your back."

Pickering lived in Lynn, about fifteen minutes north of Charlestown. Jimmy parked across the street while I went to Pickering's door alone, as I didn't want to look like a pair of federal agents come knocking. The house was an innocuous, older one-story building, sitting on a plain dirt plot a few blocks from the ocean. If this man had ever hired a landscaper, it was not evident.

I rang the bell and waited. The man who came to the door was not what I expected. Instead of the tattooed, weight-lifting ex-felon graduate of Club Fed who I was anticipating, Pickering was barely five feet tall, Caucasian, thin, wisps of grey hair combed across an otherwise balding head, unhealthy skin tone and bespectacled, looking almost exactly like my old Boston accountant. For a moment, I wondered if he was my former accountant.

"Charles Pickering? I'm Mackenzie Brody. I'm a PI working on a case dealing with a missing woman who was a friend of Thomas Costa, Junior. He's not implicated in her disappearance, but I wondered if you might have known his father, Thomas, Senior?"

"Are you with the probation office?"

"No, private. I'm working with the family."

"And why do you want to know?" Pickering asked through the screen door. His voice was strangely high pitched, and he was looking over his rectangular black framed glasses at me with raised eyebrows, as though he'd just found me cheating on my taxes. He was making me twitch already.

"I'm just trying to find out more about Thomas's family. I saw that Thomas, Senior was brought into a federal racketeering case, but the case files are sealed so I haven't been able to read them. I only saw your name on the docket as a co-defendant."

"Why don't you ask the son?" The eyebrows came down, but the frown and the screen door separating us remained.

"I spoke with him, but he wasn't especially informative."

"Well, if you saw the docket, you must know that the case was related to organized crime. I had nothing to do with that operation. I was wrongly convicted. I spent six years in confinement doing tax returns for the inmates and their families pro bono. I could have been outside running my business."

Sometimes my people reading perception amazes me. "That's great you were able to help out the inmates. Do you know why Thomas Costa, Senior was dropped from the case?"

"Word was that Costa got off because there were bigger fish. He was peripheral. I heard he took some money in and out for that night spot of his, but he had his son studying accounting and the boy had a knack for the books. My books were clean. My clients were clean. Every one of them." He said it with certainty. This was a man who apparently knew his clients very well.

109

Right, I thought, but didn't say. "Thanks for your time," I said. Pickering shut the door and just to be firm, pulled the curtain over the adjacent window.

I walked back to Jimmy and got in his car. "According to Mr. Pickering, a squeaky clean and wrongly accused ex-felon accountant, Costa was on the outside; a mob all to himself, with a son he was putting through school to learn money laundering economics for his nightclub."

"Ah. Good that there was some talent in the family," Jimmy said, starting the car.

"Morelli is next up," I said.

"I'll come in with you for that one," Jimmy said, punching Morelli's address into his navigation app.

"That probably wouldn't work well, Jimmy. He sees the two of us on his step, he's less likely to open the door. I think I'll have a better chance if I'm on my own. I'll report in, though. Just stay parked across the street. "

Morelli's residence was an old two-story clapboard house on North Beacon Street in neighboring Brighton. It looked in need of repairs. The peeling garage door was slightly askew as though an earthquake had shaken it from its hinges. I thought of things like that, being a current resident of California. More likely though, it was due to deferred maintenance rather than shakers.

As I walked up his front steps, I pulled my cell phone out of the depths of my bag and put it in the outside pocket where I could get to it fast, just in case of I don't know what. I was edgy.

"The private investigator again," Morelli said, when he answered the doorbell. "I wonder what brought you to my doorstep." He sounded as though he was attempting to be congenial. I didn't expect it to last. "Come in."

Chapter Eleven

The gusting wind that
tears and heaves the trees
in their sleep
takes as much from me.
The turbulence gives way
to a false calm,
only to be buffeted
by another chilling storm front,
as the night destroys patterns
inside and out.

I followed Morelli through the hallway and into what was ostensibly the living room, but it contained a large dining room table surrounded by too many old straight-backed chairs instead of any kind of comfortable seating. There was no evidence of a decorator's or housekeeper's touch anywhere. The window curtains were frayed on the ends. The shelves were visibly dusty. A dirty plate and cup sat on the end of a side table. The room was quiet, except for the buzzing of a fly visiting the food scraps on the plate. Morelli, himself, echoed the décor in his faded sweatpants and grubby sweatshirt. He didn't much resemble the professionally dressed educator I'd met at the City Winery. This was, apparently, the private side of him.

"Let's talk, shall we," Morelli said, signaling me to sit at the table. He moved over to the side table, opened a drawer and pulled out a semi-automatic pistol. A .45 caliber Glock, to be precise. I noticed that it was modified with a port on each side of the barrel to reduce the muzzle jump when you fired. It made for more accuracy. He sat down and put the hefty black weapon on the table in front of him with the barrel pointed in my direction. He wasn't pulling punches. My muscles tightened, but I focused on keeping still. This was not starting off well. There was a chance I could talk my way out of this, that he was just putting the heat out on the table for show.

"Don't be afraid," he said. "I won't use this. I just never know about you ex-cops. It's just insurance in case you might be carrying."

"I'm not," I replied. "I'm not a cop and have never been one."

"I'm sure I won't need it for self-defense then," he said, but his body movements signaled agitation. He kept touching his mouth with his hands and his eyes were not consistently focused. I wondered if he was high on something.

"I guess you and Costa were roommates while at school?" I thought that if I turned the questions to Costa, Morelli might settle down.

"Just for a semester. What does that have to do with anything?" he asked rather gruffly.

"I read that Professor Costa's father owned a club over in the Fenway area and maybe had some run-ins with the law. I wondered if you knew anything about that."

"Nothing that I ever heard. That's fiction. Never met old man Costa."

"I heard that Costa worked at his father's club when he was studying. Did you ever get by there?"

"Nope, I was busy getting through school. Didn't have time for clubs," he said. This line of questions was going nowhere. But I figured it would be suicide to pursue Morelli's prior insistence that he never met Sheila, and his reported stalking of her.

"Well, thanks. That's really all I wanted to ask. I guess you can't be of any help, then." I stood up, trying to keep my movements casual. He stood up at the same time, and to my relief, didn't reach for his weapon. He turned towards me as I started for the front entry. Six feet, that's all the territory I had to cover to the door.

What happened after that went by in slow motion. In spite of his heft, Morelli was fast on his feet. He stepped in front of me and put one hand over my mouth and another around the back of my neck. He pushed me with his body away from the door. I struggled in his grip, and with a flashback of having been in this position before, I had the brief thought that it was the familiarity of his acrid smell that I'd picked up at our last meeting. Morelli wasn't pushing me down on the floor this time. He dragged me across the room and tore the shoulder bag from my arm. I heard my cell phone clatter out onto the floor. He loosened one hand long enough to open a door to a set of stairs, spun me around then whipped a hand across my back, which sent me flying downstairs onto the basement floor.

I must have blacked out briefly. I sensed dark and dampness as I realized where I was and how I'd arrived there. This time I was not in my lovely Scotland. The pain in various parts of my corporeal presence was sheer at first from banging down the stairs. I'd protected my head on the way down, but at the expense of my right wrist and ribs. I laid on my side on the floor of the basement until finding myself able to make a conscious decision to move my body. Pushing myself up slowly with my left arm, I sat up, then moved my hand around on the ground near me, trying to figure out the lay of the land. There was debris on the floor. I couldn't tell what it was. Some of the room was coming into focus as there were slivers of light intersecting the room from under the door at the top of the stairs.

I don't like spiders. That was my next thought, that there must be a lot of spiders in my vicinity. I tried to shake off some of the dust, and potentially any arachnids, from my jeans and blouse.

I gave up and laid back down for a while, trying to sort out which parts of my body ached the most. A couple years of martial arts training had taught me how to curl up and roll so as to avoid injury in a fall, but nothing prepared me for a headlong dive down a dark staircase.

I could hear creaking on the floor above. Footsteps and maybe furniture being moved around. Someone would find me, I thought. Jimmy will come. I'll just wait quietly. If I scream, I'll probably get shot.

After a time, I sat up again, and tried to stand. I hit my head on a wooden rafter, which sent a volley of pain through my neck. The ceiling was about 3 inches lower than I was, and undoubtedly hosted more spiders, so I sat back on the hard dirt surface of the floor.

Looking around in the dim light, I could see what looked like garden implements leaned up against the concrete wall including a bent shovel, a rake and some other rusting tools. They were possible weapons I could use to retaliate with. I couldn't see a light switch anywhere – it was probably at the top of the stairs.

I turned slightly to see what was behind me and startled. It had the vague outline of a person, some rags hanging off a distorted shape leaning up against the back wall at an odd angle, but with no visible features. I peered closer to try and see what it was.

"Oh God," I said out loud. "Fucking bones."

I turned back around and put a mental clamp on my fear. I made a plan. I would stay quiet and wait. If the footsteps above me stopped for long enough to assume Morelli might have moved to a different room or left, I would go up the steps and try the door. If it was locked, I would get one of the garden tools and try to pry it open where the bolt was seated into the door frame.

Sitting in the semi-dark, rocking slightly back and forth and shaking, I willed my body to stop aching, and waited.

As the noise in my head started to clear, I heard a low hum in the room. It was coming from the opposite wall. I got up with the intention of exploring, in case the noise was coming from an electric panel that might offer some options for light or disrupting the house's electrical system. Keeping my head low, I shuffled carefully in that direction, cursing the loss of one shoe that had flown off when I tumbled downstairs. Part way across the room I stumbled onto the missing sneaker and gratefully slid my foot into it.

As I got closer, I made out that the hum was coming from what looked in the dim light to be a large double-door refrigerator. That gave me some hope, thinking that if I opened the doors, it would probably have internal lights that would illuminate the basement to a greater degree. The semi-darkness was spooking me as much as the bones.

I grabbed the handles with one hand on each door and pulled. They were stuck and didn't go anywhere. Pain shot through my bruised right wrist and the middle of my body from the effort. I rested a moment then put both hands on the left side door and pulled again, harder. The door gave way and light streamed out along with a bunch of plastic bags. It was the freezer I'd opened, and I jumped back as a number of heavy frozen bags tumbled onto the floor by my feet.

I saw as much as I needed to the moment I looked down. The large plastic bag on the top of the pile was frosty and cloudy, but clearly contained an intact human hand surrounded by what looked like, but obviously was not, vestiges of old frozen lentil soup. I backed away from the grisly find to the middle of the room and sat down, wrapping my arms around my legs and resting my head on my knees in shock and pain.

A burst of noise from the room above nearly knocked me over. I heard shouting, a cacophony of pounding, then gunshots. It was quiet for a few minutes, then there were more gunshots followed by a thunder of foot falls above me. The door at the top of the stairs crashed open and slammed against the wall, the sudden change of illumination hitting me like a shard of lightning.

"Boston Police," someone shouted. Another voice yelled, "Mackenzie Brody, this is the police. Are you there?" As my vision adjusted, I could see a couple of uniformed bodies looking down from the top of the stairs, then a flashlight as one of them descended.

"Yes, yes," I shouted back, tears and relief overwhelming me. I took some deep breaths. One of the cops came closer and shined the light at my face, then pulled it away quickly so as not to blind me.

"Are you injured? We have an ambulance on the way," he said.

"Various," I said, words, not sentences coming out.

"Crime scene," I said.

118

"We know you were held against your will. Morelli has been secured." he said.

"No, behind me and there," I said, pointing to the open freezer. The cop directed his flashlight over my head to the back wall and then around to the refrigerator. Immediately with his hand, he signaled the two other cops who were following him downstairs to stop where they were.

"Alright, we'll get you out of here," he said calmly.

"I can get up." He took my outstretched left hand and helped me to my feet, as we both kept our heads ducked just under the ceiling. We walked slowly up the stairs, and met another uniform at the top, who took it from there.

The living room was a shamble, with a lot of blood. Morelli's lifeless body, the source of it, was lying under the table in a twisted position on his side. His eyes were open but the side of his head, where an ear used to be, was gone. Pieces of what I assumed to be his brain and mats of hair were hanging there loosely instead. When I was ushered outside, I saw several police cruisers, lights flashing, and a SWAT truck. Jimmy and Morgan were standing just behind police tape. They were held back by the cops, but Jimmy yelled over that they would meet me at the hospital. I was invited into a waiting ambulance and ferried to the hospital.

The rest of the day was a blur of hospital staff and x-ray machines. My bag and cell phone were returned to me after Jimmy sufficiently pleaded my case that they were not part of the crime scene as they'd escaped the violence and blood spatters. Once I got my phone back, handed over from Jimmy via a kind nurse, I felt somewhat better. Funny how that happens.

After the initial medical images were assessed, I was determined to be in basically one piece. I had bruises on my side and two cracked ribs, along with miscellaneous bruises on my legs and arms from rattling down the basement stairs. My right wrist was sprained and swollen. After I was wheeled out of emergency, I was stuck in a semi-private room, curtained off from a very quiet neighbor. I wondered briefly if my roommate was alive or awaiting the coroner.

Jimmy and Morgan were allowed to visit in the evening. When they came in the room, I attempted unsuccessfully to sit up. The pain meds were kicking in. I was groggy and tired. "What took you so long to rescue me?"

Jimmy gave me his big smile. "I called the PD five minutes after you went in Morelli's door. I didn't have a good feeling. I kind of exaggerated. I said I'd heard a scream."

"You took a chance. You could have blown a good interview! Except it wasn't."

"Yes, sorry about that."

"You nearly did hear a scream when he put his customized Glock on the table. Went downhill after that."

Jimmy continued, "When the cops went to the door, he fired a round off at them through it, missing fortunately. That set the police response into high gear. One of the uniforms told me they used an infrared camera to make sure he was the only one in the living room when they busted in, but I think that was fiction. The portable version of those things can't see through walls. More than likely, they took their chances and got lucky."

"I saw the results of Morelli's losing fight. It wasn't pretty."

"Connor, when he gets wind of this, will not be amused."

"We will have solved at least one if not two of their cold cases. Chances are some of the remains were Sheila Costa's. I don't want to tell Aiden yet until forensics does their thing. I want to make sure it's not his mother."

"You won't be waiting long to talk to Aiden," Morgan added. "The PD called him, and he is on his way over from Scotland. He'll be here in the morning."

"Here comes the cavalry. Why did they contact him so fast, when there was nothing tying Morelli to Alice?"

"I got it on the quiet from one of the cops I know that there was another skeleton as well as the frozen bits you found."

"Oh Christ."

Chapter Twelve

These bends in the road
exhaust the finite strength
of one's breath,
sap the texture from hair
that is pushed back off the forehead
a thousand times,
alone on the street,
in some noisy room,
on a hillside,
in the urban fray,
beside a lake,
in a hospital bed,
or when down low behind the
freeway wheel
doing this solo thing.

There were discussions about discharging me from the hospital that night after emergency finished with me. But as it was so late and whoever needed to sign off on me was unavailable, I was treated to one night of hospitality. Detective Connor was also working late. He showed up at my bedside soon after Jimmy and Morgan left.

"Why did you pursue Donald Morelli?" Connor asked first off, standing with his arms crossed at the end of the bed.

"The fact that he lied to me that he'd never met Sheila Costa, contradicted by Sheila's letters to her daughter and Sheila having complained that he was stalking her. He also said he only knew Costa from having a few beers with him, in spite of the fact that they were roommates while they were studying. Then there was the fact of his general hatred of women. Let me think if there was anything else." I was already exhausted. I leaned back against the upraised back of the hospital bed. "That's the best I can do right now."

Connor sat down on the chair beside me, dropping his confrontational stance. "You heard that they found a second set of bones in addition to the body parts in the basement freezer?"

"Yeah, Jimmy told me. Any prelims on causes of death?"

"It'll take forensics people awhile. Both sets of skeletal remains appear to be quite a few years old. Likely not your Alice Lindsay, but we don't have information on the frozen remains yet. Is there any way I can convince you to lay off all further private inquiry related to this matter, short of exporting you back to California? This is in our hands now."

"Morelli is all yours," I said. I was warming to Connor's linguistic formalities. "I still have some interest in Thomas Costa. He has a sister who lives locally. I might want to talk to her."

"I don't care about Costa's sister. But leave Costa to me. We'll have to notify him if the remains you saw turn out to be his former wife. And we'll want to interview him as a former colleague of Morelli's. There will be some questions for him."

"You have my agreement on that." Placating the cops was not my strong point, but I could see his reasoning.

"I'll speak with you soon," he said, rising and walking out without saying goodbye.

In the morning I was discharged from the hospital on good behavior, but not before Aiden made an appearance and became a nuisance, insisting on speaking to any doctor who had anything to do with diagnosing my injuries.

"I've booked you in at the Ritz-Carlton for the next couple of nights, Mac. I've got an adjoining room. I'll keep an eye on you," Aiden said, loud enough so Jimmy could surmise who was now in charge.

I went through the discharge process with both of them and a nurse in attendance. The nurse eventually rolled me in a wheelchair out to the curb to Aiden's rental car, which was double parked and about to get towed. She helped me get in the passenger seat, then handed me a paper bag full of prescription bottles, the contents of which were supposed to allay the residual body pain. My intention was to take none of them except some over-the-counter ibuprofen.

Aiden had provided the police with a DNA sample earlier that morning in case it was needed to identify one of the bodies found in Morelli's basement.

When we got to the Ritz, Aiden unloaded his suitcase and said mine would come shortly, when Morgan sent it over to the hotel from her apartment. While the bellman took his bag to the room, we went to the hotel restaurant. My appetite was returning after a dinner of hospital food, if you could call it that. I ordered Cape Cod scallops and a margarita flatbread. I wanted to eat before the hospital pain medications wore off, which might preclude wanting further meals for a time.

"Now we wait," Aiden said. "No point in doing anything more until we know whether one of the bodies in Morelli's house is my mother's. And you need to rest and heal."

"Hopefully neither of those things will take long. A day or two. Who is looking after Erin while you're here?"

"She's staying with my cousin across the bridge in Fife. She has a daughter the same age. I don't know what the two of them do with their time on the summer break, but hopefully stay out of trouble and don't break the law."

"You don't require a detailed report from her?"

Aiden chuckled. "No, I don't. She's the one who is old enough to behave with some reason."

"And I'm not?"

"You keep getting into difficulty. That's not how this investigation was supposed to go."

"You hired me to potentially chase down a killer. I'm enough of an investigator to know that might be risky. At least I haven't been shot at this time."

"Blimey! You've been shot before? I thought you kept to white-collar criminals?"

"I was shot by a white-collar criminal. But that was a couple years ago. No big deal. It wasn't that bad."

"Apparently not," he replied, sighing.

I spent the next two days getting out of bed at the hotel only to shower as best I could with an aching body. In spite of the pain, I was enjoying having room service three times a day, ice packs delivered, and an attentive Scotsman looking after me. Meanwhile I took in the view from my 10th floor room of the area which used to be called Boston's Combat Zone. The neighborhood was considerably spruced up now from the adult entertainment venues which used to line the street. Once when I had a friend visiting Boston from out of town during a monster snowstorm, she heard a reference to the Combat Zone and thought it was where the National Guard was landing helicopters to help in the snow emergency. I don't know if the zone was named after the preponderance of crime in the area at the time, or the sailors who used to visit during shore leave. Take your pick.

By way of my published office phone number, I was receiving voice messages from various press outlets asking for interviews, since my name was referenced in the preliminary police information released on Morelli's death. As Aiden was looking for something to do, he took charge of responding to the press calls and telling them I was unavailable. He also fielded a few calls from the Boston PD. I was more than willing to delegate that duty.

Between restless naps, I made a few necessary calls, including to Carl Douglas, his wife's closure on her mother's death coming too late to benefit her. I'd already provided Douglas's contact to the Boston PD, and Carl spoke with them to offer any help he could in identifying the remains. I also took calls from Jimmy and Morgan, my cousin Jen, and from a number of my West Coast people who wanted updates on my condition, including my ex. Word had gotten around. It was a full-time job being laid up.

The call from the PD to Aiden on the initial results of the forensics on the bodies in Morelli's basement came in on the third day we were at the Ritz. Aiden knocked and entered my room after I'd gotten dressed to go down to lunch rather than order another room service.

"None of the bodies were Alice's," Aiden said, with visible relief on his face. "The remains of the body you saw were Sheila Costa's. PD has yet to identify the additional remains, but the other bones were from a middle-aged woman who died around the same time as Sheila. No news on the freezer contents, except they weren't related to me. They haven't released any other details."

"I'm so glad to hear that, Aiden. I guess I still have a job."

"The fact that Alice's body hasn't turned up doesn't mean that Morelli didn't kill her, of course, but you need to let the police do their thing to investigate. Though I expect the danger to you stopped with Morelli's death."

"Yes, good chance I'm not going to have people trying to run me down on the streets of Boston again. Or rearrange my face. I have been thinking, though, about some other threads I want to follow."

"That doesn't surprise me," Aiden said.

"Professor Costa – he doesn't get off scot-free in my book."

"Please don't bring the Scots into this."

"I promised Connor I wouldn't approach Thomas Costa, but I want to talk with Costa's sister who lives just south of Boston. When I met with Tammy Douglas's old boyfriend, he said the sister showed up at Costa's house in lieu of her brother and was pretty hostile to Sheila and her daughter. Not to mention they all got sick from her cooking. Jimmy did some background on her and according to her social media postings, she lives in Quincy. I brought her up to Detective Connor when he visited me in the hospital. He's not interested in her."

"Costa is still the only known link to when my mother went missing. We are back to square one as regards to my mother. If you want to follow up on some leads, I'll back you on that. I will stick around for a bit here in case there's any help I can provide."

"Don't you have a book to write? A daughter to monitor?"

"I'm behind on my deadlines, but that's nothing new. And Erin is at my cousin's all month and calls me daily. You don't want my help?" Aiden gave me that direct look of his, but there was mischief in his eyes.

"Your job is to sit back and pay my invoices, not peer over my shoulder," I said. Aiden folded his arms and stared at me. "It is kind of fun to have you here sometimes. But not all the time." I added.

I was discharged from the Ritz by Aiden, with some regret, the following day. Aiden kept his room there, but I insisted on moving back to Morgan's apartment to save him the expense of my accommodations at the hotel. We dropped my bags off at Morgan's apartment on the way to Quincy, a harbor town on the south edge of the Boston area.

Camila was several years younger than her brother. I'd taken a chance and phoned her to make an appointment to meet up, explaining that since I'd seen her Facebook posting, it was easy enough to look up her listed number. She accepted without much hesitation, probably curious to find out why I wanted to speak with her.

From the brief background Jimmy had done, Camila appeared to have been widowed in her thirties soon after marriage to Dennis Osterly. He died in a boating accident in Boston harbor. They had no children. She was still part-time employed as a secretary by a local manufacturing firm. She spent a lot of time on social media and gloated about accompanying her brother on occasion when he was in the UK to attend seminars or give lectures.

On the way to meet Camila, I asked Aiden to take a slight detour to drive past a house in Milton, just over the border from Quincy. The house was a Cape Cod single-story building with dormer windows upstairs, sitting on about a quarter of an acre. It had a for sale sign stuck in the grass out front. The lawn was unkempt, but the house looked freshly painted and the roof looked new.

"Why are we here?" Aiden asked, as he pulled over in front of the street address I'd given him.

"This is where Stone Hadley lived, the man who my father thought might have carjacked my brother based on his police mug shot. When he died ten years ago of an apparent suicide - in the house, by the way, the title passed to his younger brother, Irving Hadley, who never appeared to live here or rent it out as far as I could determine, but he kept it up. The title has remained with Irving, according to the property records. Irving is about sixty-nine now and owns a house in Dartmouth, Mass, where he lives by himself and works as a building and electrical contractor. He spruced this house up before putting it on the market a year ago. It's not overpriced according to the comps, but he hasn't managed to sell it. Maybe it has bad karma. Maybe it's haunted."

"Did the coppers ever search it while Hadley lived there?"

"They did get a warrant at the time and searched the place but came up empty handed. They dug up parts of the yard where there was any disturbed soil, talked to neighbors and his employer at a lumberyard, and searched the fishing boat that he owned an interest in. Again, nothing. I did my own reconnaissance inside at one point while Stone Hadley was still alive, based on a pretext of checking gas lines. The inside was pretty disheveled. He was morosely uncommunicative during the inspection."

"Do you know something about inspecting gas lines?" Aiden asked.

I laughed. "Not a clue, but I took a friend with me who worked for the gas company. He had the equipment and uniforms. We were good! But didn't get access to the whole house. Minor gas leak on the oven piping, though. We did him a favor and fixed it."

Aiden shook his head. "What a chancer you are. It's a wonder you've made it this long."

"Aiden," I said, thinking out loud. "What if Hadley was actually the culprit and my brother is buried in the basement, like Morelli's vics. No one ever investigated the basement in this house."

"I don't know if you're fixated on this because you never had any other suspects and no closure on your brother, or if you have an instinct that you should listen to. But whichever it is, I am uniquely qualified to understand it."

I took a pen and piece of paper from my bag and wrote down the phone number of the real estate agent listed on the for-sale sign. "How about we go house shopping? I think I might just want to have a look inside this adorable and possibly haunted Cape Cod."

"Right, make an appointment."

Chapter Thirteen

Life can be soft or harsh or still
or moving with a dancer's motion.
I'm inspired by their laughter,
those with lighter visions than I.
I'm down a chance street in the
confines of someone's idea.

Better to be moving, changing,
finding the balance,
so life can move
like a dance.

Camila Osterly owned a two-story house that she inherited from her parents when they died. It was about a mile back from the marina, and otherwise not unlike her brother's Cambridge home, except it was in better shape. There was a wrap-around patio along the front, with flowerpots containing geraniums arranged perfectly all along the wide railing. It looked like she'd precisely measured the distance between the pots. Not one was out of place. A small stone fountain on the front lawn was running, making a soft waterfall sound in the afternoon heat.

Aiden and I waited on the steps after ringing the bell, and Camila opened the door to greet us.

"Would you like to come in?" she asked, after our introductions.

"Yes, thank you, just for a few minutes," Aiden responded.

We followed her into the hallway, and she motioned us into a large living room with overstuffed couches and chairs, and a smattering of low bookshelves and side tables. There were a few copies of Italian Renaissance era paintings hung on the white walls and several regulation coffee table books were on the table. There was a distinct absence of personal memorabilia other than one photo on a side table of her brother in a graduation uniform, and one family portrait that showed three children and two adults, perhaps Camila, her two siblings and parents. Camila straightened her cotton print dress as she sat down primly on one of the chairs and signaled us to take positions on the couch opposite her. She was a fairly tall and large woman, with graying hair tied sharply back.

"Yes, what can I do for you this afternoon?" she said, seeming overly polite in her tone of voice and expression. Her chin jutted out, so she appeared to be slightly looking down at us. I automatically didn't trust her. People who are way too polite are usually hiding their contempt.

"As I mentioned on the phone, I'm helping Mr. Lindsay look into the disappearance of his mother several years ago, after she moved out from staying with your brother in Cambridge. We wondered if you'd ever had an opportunity to meet her during the six months she was here?" I could be polite also.

"I do recall meeting her once briefly at Thomas's house. It's been quite lonely since my husband died and my brother is all the family I have here, since my sister is overseas. It was difficult to visit him or even speak with him on the telephone when he was with Alice, though. She did not want to share Thomas."

"Did you happen to recall whether Alice had any other friends here besides Thomas?" I asked, trying to stay on neutral territory.

"None that Thomas ever mentioned. She was very obsessed with him. No offense to Mr. Lindsay, here, but she was quite the opportunist. She barged into Thomas's life and just wanted his money and his academic prestige. Thomas was certainly better off when she left, though I'm sure it was very sad for the family when she went missing. The police always thought she committed suicide, possibly because she realized the pain she had caused Thomas, distancing him from his only family." Camila smiled, lying so kindly. Passive aggressive bitch, I thought. I didn't dare look over at Aiden.

I thought I'd better steer clear of trying to refute her assertions. "Did you know Donald Morelli, one of Thomas's colleagues?" I was fishing to see if she'd read the news accounts, most of which fortunately had not included my name, of Professor Costa's friend whom she was sounding suspiciously like in her assessment of Alice.

"Oh yes of course. So tragic what happened to Don. I will attend his services. There must have been some horrible overreaction by the police to go in and kill him. I'm sure he knew nothing about those corpses the newspaper said were found in his house. I read they haven't been identified yet, but I'm sure they were there before Don bought it. Poor man. Thomas was so supportive of him. A very nice man and always so helpful." I held my tongue about how nice poor Don was being when he threw me down the stairs into a basement full of human remains and spiders.

"I read that your father owned a night club in Boston. Did the family expect the son to follow him in that business? I just wondered if it was clear early on that Thomas had such a knack for economics."

Camila perked up at the chance to heap praise on her brother. "Oh, we always knew that Thomas was a highly intelligent man who would blaze a trail to university. My father and mother did everything they could to support him. They didn't have that opportunity themselves, growing up through the time of a depression and world wars. I've had limited opportunities myself, as I've had to support myself since my husband died. Thomas helped me as much as he could and still does. He has been very generous, especially after he no longer had to support that woman or that first wife of his. Thank goodness that one left as well."

Aiden stood up. "Well, thank you Mrs. Osterly. We won't be taking up any more of your time. We'll see ourselves out." He took my left arm and gently guided me off the couch and into the hall in front of him toward the front door. I silently winced at the pain that shot through my mid-section from the movement.

"I understand you visited Thomas." Camila was talking to our backs and had raised her voice. "Stay away from him. Or there will be consequences." Neither of us looked back at her or said a word as we went out the door and down the steps. We got into the car and Aiden started the engine.

"Bloody horrible woman," Aiden said, his hands gripping the steering wheel tightly.

"I wanted to smash every one of her fucking flowerpots on the way out. I might go back there tonight with Jimmy's 9 mil and pick them off one at a time."

"No you won't, Mac."

"Yes I will, Aiden." I looked over at him and we both burst into laughter.

We continued on the drive back to Boston as I mused about Morelli and Costa's relationship and tried to get comfortable in the car. Seat belts weren't made for busted ribs. "I'd like to know more about Costa's relationship with Morelli. It seemed pretty cozy. I have an idea I want to look into," I said. I pulled out my phone and called my cousin Jen to see if she could do more research for me at the university.

I was feeling trashed by the time Aiden reluctantly dropped me back at Morgan's apartment just before dinnertime. Too much body ache, not enough pain killer. I was still holding to my over-the-counter drugs plan, with the exception of taking a sleeping pill the past couple of nights. Sleep, with two fractured ribs and various other aches, was elusive. I couldn't get comfortable in any position. I planned to have an extended happy hour with Morgan and hoped that would replace the sleeping pill. Morgan and I were wine tasting buddies from way back.

"Where do you go from here with your investigation?" Morgan asked, as she dished out a plate of steaming pasta in front of me.

"There are some avenues still to follow. I'm not giving up on chasing down Alice, dead or alive. I need to find out what happened to that woman; whether Morelli killed her or someone else did. There will be an explanation and closure for Aiden."

"He's an attractive man," Morgan said, raising her eyebrows slightly. "And he is looking out for you."

"There's something to be said for that," I said. "He is my client, which explains it."

"I see you are still the dedicated solo act, Mackenzie. Do you want the status quo to change?"

"I am doing fine living on my lovely boat when I'm not traveling and having friends like you to visit, confound and irritate whenever possible." I laughed as Morgan shook her head. Sometimes even your most complacent friends want to see you change. Good luck with that.

My happy hour plan yielded increased comfort for sleeping, and by the time I'd woken up at 9:00 AM, Morgan had already left for work at her Boston office and Jimmy was off doing some research for another client. Jen got back to me by phone, having spent the evening scouring various additional Hanford library resources.

"Your hunch was correct," Jen said. "Morelli's PhD thesis followed the outline of one of Costa's empirical studies on the economic influences of international trade that was written years earlier. I found it going through an archive of unpublished papers. It looks like either Costa wrote Morelli's thesis or handed him the substance of it."

"What about the grants? Were you able to turn up the financial crossover between them?"

"They were both applicants on several grants to the economics department for government studies. It's not clear whether they worked as a team or whether Morelli jumped on Costa's bandwagon, but they were definitely in each other's pockets as far as grants."

"What a pair," I said. "Thanks Jen. Hold onto the copies you made to show those ties. We may need them down the road."

"Alright. I hope you're feeling better, Mac. I'm here if you need me."

Chapter Fourteen

I can still taste and smell
the separation,
the hard, syncopated pulse
of losing a brother.
The deep abyss.

I felt it on my shoulders,
in my chest,
on my sandwich at lunch,
at the swings in the park,
talking to my best friend
about her loss, her brother's
death in war.

It was worse than anything
I had ever felt.
Major blues.

Aiden picked me up at noon to return to Stone
Hadley's former residence for a showing. When I'd
called the number of the real estate agent that was
listed on the front lawn sign, she informed me that it
was actually now being sold by the owner; the agency

hadn't yet taken the sign down. She gave me Irving Hadley's number and when I reached him, he agreed to meet us at the house that afternoon.

Hadley looked a lot like his deceased older brother. The resemblance was especially striking in his facial features; the high forehead, pronounced nose, and reddish complexion. The thought that he might recognize me gave me a shudder, until I remembered that I'd never met Irving; it was only Stone Hadley whom I'd met in my pretext visit to the house years before. But they were cut from the same cloth. Just to be safe, I let Aiden do the talking and did not introduce myself. The name Brody might have raised his antenna in case he'd been aware of his brother having at one time been a potential suspect in Kenneth Brody's disappearance.

"Have a look around," Hadley said, opening the door for us. He didn't offer any details or ask us any questions. He sat down at the kitchen table in front of an open beer and studied his smart phone.

We started with the upstairs, walking briefly through the two bedrooms and one bath, then came downstairs and murmured between ourselves as we went through another downstairs bedroom, bath, den and living room. There was a screen door leading to a small patio off the back of the house and an overgrown garden along a brick wall that enclosed the back yard. We headed back into the kitchen where Hadley was working on his beer, looking bored.

Aiden pulled on an inside door off the hallway that led from the kitchen into the small den. Hadley looked up briefly. "Basement. Ain't nothing down there," he said.

"I'd like to have a quick look at the basement, if that's alright. I know that flooding can be a problem around here, so it's good to have a dry basement."

"Never flooded but suit yourself."

Aiden opened the door and felt around on the side wall until he found the light switch. I hesitated to follow him, my chest tightening, but he took my left hand and led me slowly down the wooden stairs behind him. The basement door suddenly banged shut. I jumped and stifled a cry in my throat.

"It's alright, Mac. We're fine here. The door just shut on its own and there's no lock on it. I made sure of that."

The large basement under the entire footprint of the house had a 7-foot ceiling and solid concrete block walls. It was virtually barren. There was no ping-pong table, no tools, no workbench. Sections of the floor along the walls and in some of the room looked dusty and old with cracks showing in the concrete. There was a large rectangular section in the middle of the room that was smooth and looked more recently concreted.

Aiden and I walked back up the stairs. He pushed open the door and I started to breathe again.

"Like you said, not much to see down there. Where is the hot water heater?" Aiden asked.

"Round the side of the house. Same with the electric and gas meters," Hadley said, not looking up.

"That one section of the floor down there that looks like a more recent resurfacing job – was there some reason for that being done?" Aiden said. "I wondered if there has been some problem with underground piping or something."

"My brother killed himself down there, if you want to know. I repaired part of the flooring. It was a lot of years ago."

Aiden hesitated, then said. "Alright, thanks for the information. I'll give you a call if I'm interested. We've got a few more places to look at." We took our leave without further discussion.

"Are you okay?" Aiden said, once we got in the car. I was still trembling slightly.

"Let's go find a cup of tea somewhere." We got settled in a local café a few minutes later.

"Do you want something stronger than tea?" Aiden asked.

"Tea is fine, thanks. The coroner's report on Stone Hadley said that he shot himself. The police said that he was found dead in the living room. No mention of the basement in anything I read at the time. The lead detective I spoke to then also said Irving found him in the living room. He'd been dead about two days. There was no evidence of foul play."

"So, no need to repair the basement floor. Where does that leave us, Mac?"

"I've looked several times over the years through all the building permits and plans in the city file. There was no permit for construction in the basement or anywhere else since that house was built in 1946. The foundation was just concrete from what I remember of the as-built plans. Of course, there is a lot of work goes on in a house without permits."

"Why didn't the cops look into that anomaly in the basement flooring?" Aiden said. "It would seem an obvious thing to do while they were digging up the yard."

"It was never mentioned. There could have been a rug or furniture over it, so it wasn't visible at the time. The cops might have only wanted to go so far disturbing the garden, not taking a jackhammer to the foundation. They had slim justification for obtaining a warrant in the first place, since there was nothing else possibly linking Hadley to the crime except my father picking his photo out of a collection of mug shots."

"Okay. How are we going to get into that basement floor?" Aiden asked.

"I haven't figured that out yet."

"How about we see if Hadley will rent it to us for six months. What has he got to lose?"

"You are mischievous, Aiden. I don't need or want to rent a house in Massachusetts, but I like your idea. It's brilliant."

"This should satisfy your obsession in any case," Aiden said.

"No doubt trying to find what happened to my brother when he was nine and I was fourteen doesn't make sense. But someone murdered my only sibling, and by extension shattered my father. It's nothing new, this pursuit for answers. Just looking more expensive now that we're talking about real estate."

"If Irving Hadley agrees, let's contact a lawyer and set up a limited partnership for the rental so your name isn't on the paperwork," Aiden said. "I will go half with you on this, Mac."

"A partnership? You are mad enough to go into partnership with me on this? You might not want to get involved in this, Aiden. It's my thing and if I dig up the basement and there are bones in the basement, it's going to become a messy crime scene. And if there are no bones, it's still going to get crazy because Hadley is going to notice the newly poured concrete and he could get very weird about it."

"Let's not get that far ahead of ourselves. I know you want it to be true so you can finally lay your brother to rest, but it's a big if as to whether there is anything there in the basement or otherwise to nail Stone Hadley."

"I hope at least that he'll agree to rent the house, since it hasn't been sold. And instead of skeletons, we could find hidden treasure in that basement. In which case I might consider splitting it with you."

We went back to Aiden's hotel so he could make some calls. Aiden spoke to his barrister in London, who referred him to a corporate attorney in Massachusetts at an associated law firm if we needed to quickly set up a partnership. It must be nice to call your attorney at midnight local time and have him pick up the phone. I've never had that luxury.

Chapter Fifteen

Where is that child who could not sit still,
crouched in the corner of his mind until
darting and dashing about to cause
bits of trouble,
then withdrawing to observe.

He was always looking for a muddy pond
with polliwogs,
or a small hill of fresh snow,
or mice in the drain holes of the rock wall
on the way to our grandmother's.

Most of it is dim now and
bled of its mystery.
The mental pictures that remain vivid
are those that contained shock.
Those still run through my head
Like a movie I saw yesterday.

Aiden set the haunted house rental in motion,
leaving a message for Irving Hadley asking if he

would lease it for six months. I sat at the desk in his hotel suite and called Detective Connor to see how they were progressing on Morelli. He took my call this time. Maybe he wanted me to solve some more cold cases for him.

"Connor wants to meet with both of us tomorrow," I said to Aiden after the call. "Ten o'clock at Boston PD HQ."

"Alright, we'll see what he's got. But you need to leave it now, Mac. Let the cops do their job. It's likely Morelli killed my mother. I think we've got our man. I have to accept that, even if no body is ever found. I know Costa seems like an easy target, but other than having a mob connected father, an obnoxious sister, and a close relationship with a murderer, there's nothing on him."

"Lots of people have those kinds of relationships, right?" I asked. My sarcasm wasn't lost on Aiden. "I'm sorry, you are making sense and I'm probably not," I added.

"You've had an incredibly difficult few days," Aiden said, stating the obvious. I was in emotional and physical pain and close to tears, and he sensed it. "Let's go downstairs for some dinner, and then I'll drive you back to Morgan's."

Aiden drove me to Charlestown, parked and walked me up to Morgan's apartment, which was empty, as she was out. I was just as happy to crash without any further social interaction. I said goodbye to Aiden, threw some clothes off and crawled between the sheets in the guest room. I watched flickers of light from the traffic below illuminate the edges of the window curtain and tried to find a rhythm in the reoccurring red and white flashes. They were too sporadic to make sense of, but I fell asleep trying.

Aiden picked me up at Morgan's in the morning to go to Detective Connor's office at the Boston Police headquarters. Connor's office was a small pocket in a large room of cubicles. He met us in reception and ushered us back, where we sat on two hard plastic chairs beside his desk. Connor was looking good in an orderly suit and tie. He had a pleasant face in spite of his serious expression and a slightly crooked nose. He could have been a popular tv detective. If I were a casting director for a cop show, he would be my first choice.

"I can't share details of our ongoing investigation, of course, but I can tell you that the body of the second individual has been identified. She was a woman who had been arrested several times for prostitution in the Combat Zone back in the day." Aiden and I looked at each other. "The remains from the freezer are still being dealt with, but we know that the victim was female and in her twenties. She has been identified as a young woman who went missing several years ago. We're waiting to reach her family."

I started to speak but had to clear my throat and swallow before anything came out. "Cause of death been determined for any of them?" I asked.

"I can't relay all details at this time." Connor was nothing if not consistent. "But it does appear from the skeletal features that death was a result of blunt force trauma to the head on both of the older remains. We're dealing with a serial killer, and it's likely that he was responsible for Alice Lindsay's death as well."

"From the halls of an esteemed university to your desk," I said. Connor ignored my comment and continued.

"Morelli has no close relatives alive except a cousin, who we've spoken with. I just talked to Carl Douglas, whose number you provided, and also to Professor Costa again, since he is the spouse of one of the deceased. He is not a pleasant man, but we've no reason to believe at this point that he was involved. He seemed truly shocked and saddened that Morelli had murdered Sheila, and he claimed to have had no inkling that Morelli was even capable of such an act."

I chafed at his characterization. "They roomed together as students. Costa ghost wrote or assisted Morelli in preparing his PhD thesis. They were involved financially in government research grants. Morelli was demonstrably misogynistic and blamed Costa's female partners for taking advantage of his mentor. You'd think Costa would have had an inkling."

Detective Connor took a deep breath and waited to see if I was finished. "I understand where you're going with that, but as I said, we've no hard facts connecting Costa to the murders. We will continue to look for anything that might come up. I would like you to stand down from further private research and interviews along those lines or associated with Morelli, as I asked before, so as not to complicate police efforts. We're looking for any indication that Morelli was responsible for Alice Lindsay's death. Meanwhile, we have a serial killer, he's dead, and you're very lucky you were not another one of his victims." Connor sounded like he was rehearsing the report he was about to write his superiors describing how he shut down PI Mackenzie Brody's private investigation.

"You have our agreement on that," Aiden interjected. "I wish you luck on your investigation, and please keep me informed if anything comes up pointing to the disappearance of my mother."

We left the station and headed back to the Ritz. Every bruise and crack I had acquired via Donald Morelli was hurting.

"I know you were frustrated by his speech," Aiden said as we were driving. "But you did well to keep it in check. I'm beginning to be able to read your moods."

"As long as you can't read my mind, Aiden. You don't want to go there." The vision of the gristly frozen body parts landing at my feet kept finding its way into my head. Knowing now that it was a young woman who suffered that fate made it even more gruesome and sad. That memory was going to take some time to process.

Aiden and I stayed in his Ritz suite, focused on working out the logistics of attempting to rent Stone Hadley's old house so we could have a closer look at the basement there.

Aiden ordered room service and I downed a martini with lunch. It seemed to help. After the meal,

as I was having trouble focusing on anything
including keeping my eyes open, Aiden showed me
to the bedroom to take a nap. When I woke up later
in the afternoon, he was working on his laptop in the
living room of the suite. He drove me back to
Morgan's before dinnertime, where I promptly went
to the guest room and fell asleep again, skipping
dinner.

By the end of the day, Hadley still had not
responded to two phone calls from Aiden. Later that
night, Stone Hadley's house burned to the ground.

Jimmy met me at the breakfast table at Morgan's
when I got up. Morgan was dishing up scrambled
eggs and toast for the three of us. He'd received a
media alert on one of his news websites for articles
referencing Hadley, and it turned up a hit about the
Hadley property in Milton becoming fully engulfed at
9:00 PM the prior evening. The article stated that no
one lived there at the time therefore there were no
injuries. The cause of the blaze was unknown but was
being investigated by the Milton Fire Department.

"Dammit to hell, Jimmy!" I'd kept Jimmy
apprised of my efforts to investigate the basement in
Stone Hadley's old house. "You have a contact in the
arson department in Boston, right? Can you ask what
are the chances that remains buried under a concrete
floor might survive a structure fire over it?"

"Yes, I'll get in touch with him and also see who
he knows at Milton Fire. If we play our cards right,
this might work in your favor. If we alert their arson
investigator to the fact that the former owner was

once a person of interest in your brother's disappearance, they might agree to dig up what's left of the basement while they are poking around looking for the ignition source."

Aiden wasn't exactly overjoyed about the news when I phoned him from the breakfast table, but he did seem relieved that the ball was now ostensibly in the fire department's court. "We'll see how it plays out, Mac."

I spent the next two days doing some further recuperation at Morgan's while she and Jimmy were out working. In between resting, walks, and dinners with Aiden, I was online answering emails and touching base with a couple of other clients about possible future work. I still had a business to run and there would be, hopefully, life after this case.

My current client, except for our dinners out, was chilling his heels at the Ritz and working on his next book. He would not tell me what it was about and said that before he would give me any details, I had to read the first two novels in the series about a mole in MI6. That would take me some time.

Jimmy obtained some intelligence from his fire department contacts the following morning and arranged to meet up with Aiden and myself for lunch. Aiden picked me up at Morgan's and Jimmy met us at the restaurant at the Park Hyatt, where we took a table in a quiet and empty corner of the room.

"I'm sorry I can't have you speak with my fire department contact directly, Mac, but he didn't have the authority to talk to me about what they found, and he wasn't comfortable widening the circle."

"No problem, Jimmy. What's the bottom line?"

"The cement floor in the basement was intact when they could safely get to it. It took some clearing first – the house looked like a wildfire had engulfed it, leaving mostly only the chimney standing. They turned up the middle section of the concrete that you described. Nothing. No bones. They did a careful job of it, that he guaranteed me. There was nothing to find. Maybe it had been re-poured at some point because the concrete had failed in that section."

I was not aware that I had been holding my breath while Jimmy spoke, until after he finished. I exhaled. "I can't figure out why Irving Hadley told us that his brother had committed suicide in the basement, when according to the police, Stone shot himself in the living room. Why didn't Irving just say that he'd fixed the concrete down there?"

"Jimmy, what did the fire department determine was the cause of the fire? Was it suspicious?" Aiden asked.

"They haven't completed their investigation yet, but off the record I was told it's looking like an insurance torch job. Whether they can prove it or not is another thing. The source of ignition was apparently wiring in the living room walls. But Irving Hadley was a building contractor who had an electrician's license, as you said. He could have made it look good."

"I wonder what reason he would have had to torch it, if there was nothing to hide?"

"Maybe he didn't want to bother renting it. It hadn't sold. The market isn't great. Could be a lot of things, including the fact that his brother did commit suicide in that house. He may have wanted it gone and out of his life or an insurance payout," Aiden responded.

"Or possibly Irving was telling us the truth; that his brother did actually die in the basement and it required some clean up and repositioning of the body to make it appear a suicide," I said.

Jimmy added, "There's that, but there's an alternate possibility as well; that someone else died in the basement, requiring some clean up, but the body was buried elsewhere."

Chapter Sixteen

In front of one's eyes, life sways
from the safe and familiar chorus
to the frightening unknown,
playing out the spiritual lines
in the universe's half-way zone.

It's not a true world.
There are only true hearts,
that need constant care
to resolve the counterpoint.

Aiden and I drove up the Massachusetts coast the next morning to give us both a break from an emotionally exhausting week. There is no coast road that winds all the way up north, but you can drive straight up toward New Hampshire for an hour on Highway 1 or Interstate 95 and peel off toward the coast in many places. We exited the freeway a few miles south of the Mass border and turned east a few more miles to the town of Newburyport.

We parked in a lot behind Newburyport's main street and walked over to the path along the Merrimack River, which emptied out into the North

Atlantic. We wandered past the old Custom House Museum and along the fishing boat docks toward the Coast Guard Station. Aiden was unusually quiet.

"The Coast Guard, which was founded here by the way, has a lot to do on the Merrimack. The mouth of the river is tough to navigate because of the tidal changes." I said, as we walked.

"It reminds me of a lot of small river towns in the south of England, like in Devon along the River Exe. Would you ever consider moving from LA?" he asked. "I know you love living on the water there, but you have deep connections elsewhere. And there are such beautiful places on the water that are not also desert, or fire and earthquake prone."

"Your side of the ocean is always calling me, Aiden. But on the plus side for California, there are twelve months of boating per year. When I come to the East or the other side of the Atlantic in the fall or winter and see the boats wrapped up in white plastic in the boatyards, I grieve for their owners."

"You have a point there. How about places like Florida or the Caribbean?"

"Sorry, don't like tropical climates. Bugs, sweat and stuff."

"You are a hard one to please."

"I admit to hardly ever being content," I said.

We returned to the car and drove out to Plum Island to see the sunset over the dunes. We stopped in the small local convenience store on the main drag, and Aiden bought me a baseball cap that said 'PI' on it, to wear on my next surveillance, he said. We stopped for dinner at the Plum Island Grill and sat at the bar for a glass of wine and some food.

"We need to check out Irving Hadley's house on the south shore. There are a lot of unanswered questions, but what if…" I started, as we sat outside on a bench after dinner and waited for the sun to go down.

"What would you expect to find there, Mac?"

"I don't know. I just have a feeling. My emotions on this are a mess. This is ancient history, practically. Or at least it was until a few days ago."

"I can appreciate your feelings, but without a good reason to go after Irving Hadley, you might just be prolonging your agony."

"I can do it on another trip here, Aiden. Sorry, I don't mean to involve you in all this personal stuff."

"How Stone Hadley died and whether in fact his brother or someone else killed him downstairs, then dragged him up to the living room and made it look like suicide, or why Irving might have burnt the house to the ground could be totally irrelevant to you finding out what happened to your brother. You're operating on pure speculation that may have no basis in reality."

"And you're telling me that?" Aiden registered the irony and laughed.

The drive back to Boston took under an hour. Aiden dropped me at Morgan's and said we'd meet up tomorrow to make some kind of plan to check out Irving Hadley's house in Dartmouth. I also had some research to do online about his background.

It sounds perhaps unsettling to admit that one has a good time looking into the details of another person's life in the online public record, but I find it intriguing. If you've done it enough times while trying to find people or researching backgrounds for various types of cases, you get to the point where you can see past the raw data. Having read thousands of reports during years of investigations, you know what types of data to take with a large grain of salt, as it might be partially or wholly incorrect. From former addresses and telephone numbers to lists of possible employers, litigation, debt or relatives, the online record is rife with inaccuracies, which is one reason why the Fair Credit Reporting Act exists. PI's do not have access to law enforcement databases such as the National Crime Information Center or even the Department of Motor Vehicles records in many states, so we have to work around it. But familiarity with the process of research breeds a kind of second sense and a hawk's eye for inconsistencies. You learn what public information to trust or not, and you can read between the lines.

According to his online public record, Irving Hadley had a checkered past. The types of records he was hitting on in the search indexes were those that could be confirmed as accurate because recent court documents were accessible online. He had no social media presence at all, but he had numerous run-ins with law enforcement and civil courts. He lost his contractor's license after being sued several times for contract disputes over the past ten years. He had a conviction for driving under the influence and possession of a firearm three years ago, after which he got off for time served and probation. He had a long list of traffic violations and tax liens. It looked like his driver's license was suspended, although that information may not have been up to date. And he had a temporary restraining order filed on him just the year before by a construction business partner with whom he got nasty.

The list of potential relatives and associates that turned up online for Hadley were probably mostly inaccurate. But all said, Irving Hadley's life was not a pretty picture. I had an idea where to look for at least some anecdotal information on him to fill out the profile; Stone Hadley's former fishing buddies.

There were two fishing pals of Stone's whom I'd reached during my past investigations, that had allegedly been fishing offshore with Stone on the day that my brother was carjacked. Both had vouched for Stone's presence, giving him an alibi. I dialed both of them; the first was disconnected but a man answered the second number.

"Frank Poulter?" I asked, when the first call was answered.

"Who is this?"

"Mackenzie Brody. We spoke some years back when I was looking into my brother's disappearance many years ago. You provided the police with an alibi for Stone Hadley at the time."

"Yeah, that was a bunch of years ago. Why are you calling now?"

"You may have heard that Stone Hadley's old house in Milton just burned down. Irving owns the property now."

"I know about that. What has that got to do with anything," he said, sounding annoyed.

"I wondered if you knew what kind of relationship Stone had with his brother?"

"They were brothers, that's all I know."

"Did Irving go fishing with you guys as well?"

"I don't remember."

"Is your other partner, that guy Jake, still around?"

"He's still alive, if that's what you mean. Don't know where he is. And I have no reason to talk to you." Poulter hung up the phone. So much for that line of inquiry.

Not one to be put off easily, I decided to go looking further for fisherman number two, whose old phone number was no longer connected. At least Jake Pirro was still above ground, if Frank was telling the truth. I couldn't find another working phone or a current address for Pirro, but luckily his fishing boat was documented with the United States Coast Guard, and that's a public record. A quick search of the web pulled up the location of his marina, referenced in a recent article in a regional paper of him landing the biggest catch in a local tournament.

Pirro's fishing boat, Lady Jane, was in a marina south of Boston Harbor, sheltered from the Atlantic by breakwaters in Quincy Bay. As Aiden and I were planning to drive that direction in the afternoon, I asked him to pick me up earlier so that we could stop at the marina.

Finding Lady Jane's wet slip was a piece of cake. After we parked, I walked down to the docks and asked a couple of guys who were washing boats where she was and got a fast answer. The wind had picked up and the dock workers were securing boat covers against the gusts.

"How about you stay here, Aiden, and I'll walk down to the slip?"

"You don't want backup? Seems you always need it."

"I don't always need it. I'll be right back," I said, walking off down the ramp, leaving him standing by the railing at the edge of the docks. I wasn't about to take no for an answer.

Lady Jane was a forty-foot sport fishing boat with inboard motors and tall tuna towers looming over her deck. The thought of sitting way up there with a rod in hand while the boat rolled in the swells was not something I could imagine doing for the sake of catching a fish. In fact, you couldn't pay me to do it. The boat was about twenty years old by the looks, but well maintained. I walked around on the dock near her stern as spray from the wind gusts put a sheen on her hull. An older man was kneeling on the dock beside the boat, untying a line from a cleat. It looked like he just about to take her out.

"Jake Pirro?"

He looked up and took off a floppy hat that was covering his white bald head, which apparently hadn't seen much sun recently, but had so many brown spots it reminded me of a decayed apple. He wore grungy overalls, gloves and work boots. There were some dark red blood stains on his overalls. Fish blood, I had to assume.

"You lookin' for a charter?"

"No, I was hoping to talk to you about one of your old fishing buddies."

"Who would that be?"

"Stone Hadley. We talked on the phone a lot of years ago about him. You might not remember."

"Oh yeah, I remember. You're the private eye with the dead brother. Still nosing around, trying to put a nail in Stone's coffin?"

"My brother's disappearance is still unsolved. I was in the area, so thought I'd see if you were at the marina." Pirro busied himself with the dock lines and didn't respond, so I tried another tactic.

"Lady Jane is a beautiful boat. Looks like you've taken great care of her," I said. Boaters like it when you compliment their vessels, so I hoped it would soften the glare he was giving me. It didn't.

"How'd you find me?"

"Talked to Frank Poulter. He thought you might be around." That was vague and stretching the truth, but I wasn't outright lying.

"Well maybe you can fuck off," he said. I backed up a step as he walked close past me and hopped over the stern into the cockpit. He smelled vaguely of dead fish.

"I heard that Stone killed himself in the house." Pirro stood at the helm, not speaking. He flicked a switch. I heard the engine room blower start up. It

162

was a standard safety procedure to air out the engine compartment of potential fumes before starting inboard engines. "Did his brother fish with you guys?"

"Sometimes. So what?"

"Just wondered. You heard the house just burned down?"

"No great loss."

"Had you ever been to his house?" Pirro didn't answer the question.

"You wanna talk more, you're gonna have to get in the boat. Takin' her out for a spin to test the engines."

I hesitated, calculating the risks of being alone at sea with this unpleasant stranger.

"Too scared? Stepping off land scares the crap out of most women." In response, I put one foot on the gunwale and jumped over into the boat. I stood in the cockpit while he turned over the twin engines, and a thin plume of black smoke was emitted from a stern vent. "Goddamned starboard engine," he said.

While Pirro put the dual helm controls into reverse to take her out of the slip, I pulled out my phone and texted Aiden. "Going for a quick ride. All ok. Back soon." I put the phone away before I could see his response.

Lady Jane lurched as Pirro spun her around to exit the marina and head out into Quincy Bay. He revved the engines and kicked up the speed. The boat bounced in the swells. I put a hand on the gunwale to steady myself. Pirro had his back to me as he stood at the helm.

"I wondered if Stone Hadley had a gun." I said, talking louder over the engine noise. I just came out with it. I don't know what I was expecting him to say.

Pirro turned to answer me. "Stone wasn't into guns. Irv was the one with guns. Irv and me both." Seemed like he added that last to frighten me. So far, it wasn't working.

"That's strange. I heard Stone shot himself. Not a good way to go."

"Yeah, well no way is a good way to go. You got that?" I wasn't sure what he meant. He looked at me and then leaned over and spat into the churning water.

"You think Stone killed himself?" I knew I was pushing it, but sometimes you have to. Pirro didn't respond. He increased the boat's speed and put her broadside to the swells, which were increasing the further we got out from the shore. It was not the way to smooth the ride in rough water. Lady Jane pitched against the waves, nearly knocking me off my feet. I sat down on the bench beside the helm and held on. It was clear he was attempting to freak me out.

"I dunno, what do you think?" he shouted over the engines. "You ask a lot of fucking questions." Pirro brought the helm levers up further. It felt like we were pounding around at about 20 knots. I could hear things falling off the shelves down in the cabin. Spray was hitting me in the face and soaking my hair. The motion of the boat didn't make me seasick, but my ribs were complaining from the erratic movement. It was not the way I would have treated my boat or my passengers. Not even to make a point. Especially not to test someone's nerve.

The next thing Pirro did shocked me even more. He left the helm, climbed up on the deck and made his way up the tuna tower. He'd left the helm on auto pilot, and we were safely on a course between a couple of the small islands in the bay but heading in a direction that looked to cross the ferry traffic lane at a right angle, with a ferry heading our way. Pirro sat up in the tuna tower and laughed.

"I'm glad you're amused," I shouted up at him. I held on against the rocking motion of the boat and calculated that we had probably five minutes before the steaming ferry would get close enough to cause alarm. Pirro had no engine controls in the tower. He'd have to come down. And I knew he would do so at the last possible minute to save his boat from crashing into the ferry. I waited, my advantage being that I knew something about boats, and he didn't know I knew about boats.

Just as the ferry operator sounded the universal danger signal of five short blasts on his horn, warning us that we were on a potential collision course, I grabbed the helm controls and wheel and swung the boat hard to port, gunning the engines to get us away from the collision trajectory and to the stern of the ferry. Pirro had just started to climb down from the tower at that moment, and the motion almost threw him off the tower. He cursed as his feet dangled in the air, clung on to the tower with one arm, then slowly got his footing and came down.

"Sorry about that," I said, as I slowed the engines down while the ferry left us in its wake. I turned the helm over to him. He swung the wheel and pointed the bow toward home.

"Sit your goddamned ass down and shut the fuck up," he said. I turned away from him so he wouldn't see me smile.

Pirro brought Lady Jane back into the marina at a reasonable speed. I hopped off as he slowly entered the slip and I put the dock lines over the bow and stern cleats while he shut down the engines.

"I think you'd best get off my dock now," he said.

"Right," I replied. "Thanks for the ride," I said over my shoulder. Jake Pirro watched me walk away up the dock.

Aiden was waiting for me at the end of the ramp, looking very irritated. "I didn't need backup. I'm completely fine," I said, when I reached the top. He looked at my damp clothing and hair and shook his head.

"I think there's a towel in my bag in the boot," he said.

We drove south toward Dartmouth, stopping for lunch on the way at a café in Padanaram, a small coastal village on Apponagansett Bay. We discussed the fact that I had no plan other than to just have a look at Irving Stone's house.

"Maybe we'll see that it's for sale and we can buy it," I announced, as we walked along Gulf Road after lunch, lingering in the sun, giving me a chance to dry out. The bridge that spanned the bay was populated with sailboats at moorings on either side, separated by a drawbridge. This was my kind of town.

"This is getting more expensive as we go," Aiden said.

"Just kidding. It hasn't escaped me that he possibly burned down Stone's old house the minute someone wanted to rent it. He likely wouldn't sell his house to us. And we'd have to set up a shell corporation to purchase it."

Aiden laughed at my fiction. "Well let's drive by it in any case. Then perhaps you'll come up with some more hairbrained ideas."

Irving Hadley owned a two-story clapboard sided house on Allen Street with an attached one car garage on about a half an acre of land. There was an old car in the driveway that had seen better days and overgrown shrubs practically obscuring the concrete walkway from the cracked concrete drive to the front door. There wasn't much room on the street to pull over in front of it, but Aiden stopped the car on the verge just beyond Hadley's house. Aiden suddenly swung his arm out across my chest at the same time that a pick-up truck crashed into the back of our car and stopped. "Christ. Saw that coming in the rearview. Are you ok?" he said.

Before I could answer, the motor of the truck behind us revved, and the truck began pushing our car forward.

"Get us out the hell out of Dodge!" I yelled. Aiden threw the car into drive and jammed his foot down on the pedal. Our car surged forward as he steered it out into the road. The truck disengaged from our bumper as we pulled out, but seconds later, came bearing down on us again. This time I was able to turn around and start taking a video with my phone and get a look at the driver. It was Irving Hadley.

The truck bore down on us again as Aiden turned onto a neighboring rural road that was wide open. Hadley tried to keep up, but his truck was no match for the rental SUV. With some full steam ahead driving, Aiden lost him when we turned onto Route 6, heading away from New Bedford and past the University of Massachusetts complex. Aiden turned on Route 24 and pulled over to have a look at the damage to the back of the car.

"You ok?" I had my arms wrapped around my mid-section, which hadn't taken kindly to the sudden movements.

"I will be. Give it a few. Been a rough day for my ribs."

Aiden got out and walked around the car. "It's drivable," he said. "Let's pick up the freeway to Boston and then have a word with the police, the rental company and my insurance company."

We drove directly to the Ritz, and Aiden started making phone calls. He reported the incident to the Dartmouth Police Investigations Division, and the detective he spoke with said he would file it as a road rage incident, pending any further evidence of a criminal attack. Aiden explained that the situation was more complicated than that, but he would refrain at the moment from coming to the station to register a criminal complaint, since neither he nor his passenger were injured. The insurance company, after Aiden sent them the incriminating video identifying Hadley's truck, was going to coordinate with the rental company. Since the car was fully insured, they would provide Aiden with a new rental while the rest was sorted out, including their attempt to go after Irving's insurance for the damages.

I called Detective Connor of the Boston PD and left a message that I would like to speak with him about a situation unrelated to Morelli or Professor Costa and Costa's killed and or missing partners.

"What else can we do for fun today?" Aiden said, when we both finally got off our phones.

"You haven't had enough yet? Because I can think of a few things," I said.

"Well, maybe better not. How about martinis and dinner?" he suggested. That was a welcome idea. We headed down to the hotel restaurant.

When we got settled with drinks and menus in front of us in a corner booth at a widow overlooking the Boston summer evening, Aiden looked at me quizzically.

"What?" I asked.

"What does 'get the hell out of Dodge' mean?" I laughed for the first time that day. "I got your meaning, but the phrase eluded me," he said.

"Dodge City? Kansas? Does that mean anything to you?"

"Not a scrap."

"Sorry. Didn't you ever watch any old westerns? It's a wild west horse opera idiom. Hollywood. It's like saying 'Get the fuck out of here,' but in a John Wayne sort of way."

"That explains it," he said.

Detective Connor called me the next morning and agreed to meet Aiden and I at the Ritz for a discussion.

Connor met us in the restaurant while Aiden and I were having breakfast. I flagged a waiter and ordered the detective some coffee.

"I hope you haven't been causing more disturbances," Connor said, as he sat down.

"I wanted to talk to you about another cold case."

"This sounds like a problem already," Connor said, looking from me to Aiden. He stayed put though. That was a good sign. Maybe he was beginning to appreciate me in some small way.

"It's about the disappearance of my brother about twenty-five years ago. The carjacking happened in Boston and was handled by your people. Detective Banning was the lead on it, but he retired about ten years ago and has Alzheimer's now."

"Thank you for the update on one of my former colleagues, Ms. Brody," he said dryly. "What happened?"

I went through the scenario with Conner and explained my father's possible ID of Stone Hadley from a mug shot, my investigative attempts over the years, as well as visiting Stone Hadley's old house, the house burning down, and what happened when we pulled up outside Irving Hadley's Dartmouth house the day before. He listened, at least.

"It must have gotten back to Irving that I talked to Stone's old fishing mates enquiring about him, and he connected the dots on who was trying to rent the house. Irving may know more about his brother's actions that might relate to my brother."

Connor looked back and forth between his coffee and me. "What would you like me to do?" he said. "I can't re-open the case again based on what you've told me. Stone Hadley is long dead and there is no evidence that Irving Hadley knows more about your brother's case. You may have just irritated the hell out of him."

"What if the Milton Fire arson team determine that the house was a torch job?" I asked. "If you could coordinate with the fire department and get an opportunity to interview him, perhaps some useful information would come from it. After that road rage incident, I can't help but think I touched a nerve with him."

"If it will keep you out of the picture, I will attempt to follow up with them and see what can be done."

"Just as an aside, Detective, Stone Hadley's old fishing partner, Jake Pirro, said that Stone didn't have guns. Irving was the one with the guns."

Detective Connor looked thoughtful, briefly, then summarily drained his coffee and left us. He wasn't one for long goodbyes.

"Connor owes me a favor," I said, after he'd left. "I'm not sure he sees it that way, but at least he's going to try to help."

The phone call from Connor to my cell phone came in not two hours after we'd parted. We were in

Aiden's suite at the Ritz. I put the call on speaker so Aiden could hear.

"Ms. Brody, the Dartmouth Police went by Irving Hadley's house after receiving reports from his neighbor of the sound of gunfire. Hadley didn't respond and they entered the premises. Hadley was found dead from a gunshot to the head. It's being treated as a possible suicide."

I looked at Aiden, at a loss for words.

"There's more. Brace yourself for this one," Connor added.

"There was a possible suicide note left behind, ostensibly in the handwriting of Irving Hadley. It read, 'I didn't mean to kill the boy. He didn't suffer.'"

I closed my eyes and tried to process the words, but I couldn't quite register the information. I was silent. Aiden gently took the phone from my hand.

"This is Aiden Lindsay. Thank you, Detective Connor. Please let us know where this goes from here."

"The premises are being searched. I will let you know right away if they find anything," Connor said. "This will likely take a couple of days, but Dartmouth will move on it quickly while the scene is fresh."

"Let's take a walk, Mac," Aiden said, after he hung up the call. He got up immediately from the table and I picked up my bag. We went down through the hotel lobby and out into the streets of Boston. The expansive green gardens of Boston Commons were just a block from the hotel. We crossed Tremont Street and walked silently along the park paths wandering through the lush grounds toward the Frog Pond. The park was sparsely populated, it being a workday, with just a few tourists. The heat and humidity felt suffocating, relieved only by the shade of the trees.

As we meandered on the paths, I stated the obvious. "Irving Hadley looked like his brother. My father identified Stone from the mug shot because of their resemblance. Irving was the one with the guns. It was Irving all along."

"That seems to be the case, Mac. I can postpone my trip back to Edinburgh for a few days. I imagine you'll want to be here longer?"

"I want to see what turns up in their search. I hope they find Kenneth's remains so I can have a proper burial for him. You don't need to stay. You're my client. This isn't your case."

"Yeah, client. Maybe a bit of a partner too." He took my hand as we walked, while quiet tears ran down my face.

"'The boy didn't suffer.' What the hell does that mean?" I asked. "Was he was shot in my father's car, then dragged off by Irving Hadley back to his house while still alive and finished off there while in utter terror? Or did he die after being shot in the car and Hadley took his body to his house to bury before ditching the car? We're never going to know the answer to that now."

"Try not to imagine the worst, Mac."

"I will try. But there's the tendency to try and fill in the vacuum. You know?"

"I know exactly what you mean."

"Sorry. I don't usually get this distressed. He died a long time ago."

"It's okay, Mac. You've been attacked twice in the course of my mother's investigation, and you're still recovering from your interactions with a serial killer. It has been a rough couple of weeks. Give yourself a break."

"Yeah, seems like the lack of closure on the death of someone you love tends to make the loss fester. You've been dealing with the same thing with your mother, just more immediate."

"We'll both get through this," he said.

We crossed Charles Street and walked over by the swan boat dock, where a couple of actual swans were swimming around the plastic swan-themed tourist vessels. A boat full of adults and kids drifted past, the sounds of the children's excited voices carrying over the water.

"My mom and dad used to bring Kenneth and I here when we were little. I always made a nuisance of myself because I wanted to drive the boat."

"I see. Incorrigible captain from a young age," Aiden said.

We wandered back to the Ritz and spent a quiet afternoon. I curled up on the suite's couch with a book and he sat at his laptop and worked.

My default method for processing loss has always been to let it into my psyche in small bits over time, so as not to be overwhelmed by it. To have dealt with the loss of a sibling once and then be faced with the certainty of it twenty-five years later was beyond my capacity to swallow all at once. It would have to come in bits.

Chapter Seventeen

My father's generation and his father's
and his father's
were stalked by war.
We are likewise haunted
foot soldiers,
but in a strange world now where
everyone's war
comes to our media doorstep
in digital form.

There are still boot prints in the sand,
spent shells on the grieving ground.

Aiden dropped me off at Morgan's apartment in the early evening. She ordered in dinner from a local Japanese restaurant and then we watched some mindless tv. I didn't feel like talking, I just wanted to be in the company of a friend and not think. Morgan knew that drill, having had trials of her own in past years, when I was sometimes able to be that anchor for her. I went to bed early.

At 9:00 AM as I was putting on make-up after a shower, my cell phone buzzed with a call from Detective Connor.

"The Dartmouth PD confirmed the suicide note was in Irving Handley's handwriting. And they found remains buried in Hadley's backyard consistent with a young male," Connor said. "I'll give you the number of the Dartmouth team and you can arrange to give them a DNA swab to assist with confirming the victim's identity."

"Thank you, Detective Connor. Did they say whether it looked like the body had been there for a lot of years?"

"Yes, no confirmation until forensics has done their thing, but it appeared as though the victim was buried there some time ago, and probably died from a gunshot wound to the chest. They're also revisiting Stone Hadley's apparent suicide, and whether Irving Hadley could have been behind it."

Morgan had left for work, and I shuffled around the quiet apartment for a few minutes after speaking with Detective Connor. I called Aiden, who picked up on the first ring.

"It's likely him, Aiden. Remains of a young male found buried in the yard. I have to go to Dartmouth this afternoon to give them a DNA sample to confirm. Prelim cause of death is gunshot wound to the chest."

"I'm so sorry, Mac. I'll drive you down there if you want."

"Thanks, yes. The handwriting analysis was positive as well for Irving's suicide note. I can only hope to God that Kenneth died quickly and wasn't consumed with fear and loneliness being on his own to face death at nine-years-old."

"He's at peace now. And has been for many years."

"It's just this delayed grief."

"I know," Aiden said. "You carry it with you, but you'll be alright."

We returned to Dartmouth that afternoon so I could provide a DNA swab to the forensics team conducting the investigation. On the way back to Boston, I suggested we drive by Costa's sister's house again. I wanted to get back on track with Alice Lindsay's investigation, if only to give myself a reprieve from the cascade of emotions I was feeling about my little brother's murder.

As we pulled up across the street from Camila Osterly's house, she was standing on the porch bent down over one of her flowerpots, gardening gloves on her hands. She didn't look up at our car.

"I'm going to talk to her. See what other lies she has to tell me," I said. I released my seat belt. Before I could open the door, Aiden grabbed my left arm.

"Don't, Mac. There's nothing to be achieved by that right now."

"I don't like or trust that woman. What did I tell you about trying to micromanage me on this investigation? I'm the private eye, you're the client."

"That's what you tell me. But enough excitement for the moment?"

"Yeah, well maybe," I said. I slowly refastened my seat belt and sat back in the seat, wincing from a sharp pain in my gut. Aiden started the car and put it into gear. Camila looked up as we were pulling away. I met her glance, then turned to focus on the road ahead.

We stopped at a small café near Charlestown on the way to Morgan's. We sat outside on the stone patio at a small round metal table bearing a jar candle that flickered dimly and smelled of vanilla. I ordered up tea and a sandwich, not being in the mood for much more of a meal. Visiting flies ate more of the meal than I did.

"I'll notify my father, if they confirm the bones are Kenneth's."

"Will you go see him?" Aiden asked.

"Yes. I won't phone first and ask him or the staff if he wants to see me, I'll just go there. He needs to hear it from me, not from the police. Even if he doesn't want to see me or if he doesn't remember who I am."

"I get that. Do you want company?"

"Best on my own, Aiden. Thanks though. What do you remember about your dad? Was he there much for you as a kid?"

"I don't remember a lot. He was gone before I was five. He smelled like cigarettes. Cigarettes and cigars. I recall that. Heavy smoker. Probably lead to his early demise."

"Did they have a good marriage? Alice was single a lot of years after that. Odd that she didn't remarry."

"She always spoke lovingly about him to us. At one point when I was a teenager, I asked if she was

179

looking to get married again. She said she was too busy taking care of two kids and holding down a job. More concerned about family than herself."

"She sounds like a kind soul, Aiden. I'm glad you had her to raise you and Sandra."

"Yes, that doesn't change, whether she's alive now or not."

The call came in the following morning from Dartmouth PD confirming that the remains found in Irving Hadley's backyard were those of nine-year-old Kenneth Brody, confirmed from old dental records in his archived police file, as the DNA results were taking longer. It would be some days before their investigation was complete and the coroner would release his bones to a local funeral home. I made preliminary arrangements for Kenneth to be interred next to my mother's grave, and I planned to return to Massachusetts for the burial.

Morgan went out-of-town that morning to attend work meetings in Chicago and left me the keys to her car for the drive to visit my father.

The assisted living facility where my dad had resided for the past half dozen years was in Topsfield, Mass. The town was about an hour drive from Charlestown, up Interstate 95. When I got there, I showed my ID, explained the circumstances, and was duly led to my father's room. The caregiver on duty advised me not to expect much. He rarely left his room, and his dementia was progressing. When I went in, he was dressed, sitting on a small sofa next to the bed, staring vacantly at a tv that was on without sound. He had a few more facial wrinkles but the same full head of gray hair as the last time I'd seen him. Needing a trim though.

"Dad, it's Mac," I said, kneeling in front of him to get at his eye level.

"Who's Mac?" he said, putting a hand up to scratch his chin as though he was only asking himself and giving it some thought.

"I'm your daughter. Mackenzie."

"Didn't know I had one." His tone was gentle, not like previous visits when he was sometimes gruff and asking me to leave within minutes of arrival. I didn't know if he was chilling out due to the advancement of the dementia, or some other change of life.

"You've always had a daughter, and I'm it. I want to talk to you about your son, Kenneth. My brother. He was kidnapped when he was nine. We were both there." His demeanor changed slightly. He gazed down at the side table and picked up the tv remote. He spoke without looking at me.

"He's dead, isn't he?"

"Yes, Dad. He died a long time ago. But I kept looking for him. I found the man who took him, who was responsible for his death."

"I'm sorry. I lost him."

"Wasn't your fault, Dad. I've told you that a million times." I reached for his hand and held it. He let me this time.

"You were right all along. The guy who you saw in the mug shot, who you thought took him. It was his brother. They were a lot alike. That's how I found

181

him. You found him." My dad kept looking away, but he stroked my hand a few times, tentatively, with his other hand.

"The man who took your son is dead. We get to bury Kenneth now. I'm going to bury his bones next to Mom's. Soon as we can. In a couple weeks. I want you be with me when I do that."

My father glanced up at me and smiled. He didn't seem to notice my tears. He didn't say anything.

"I'll see you soon, Dad." I got up, leaned over and hugged him. Then I left.

Aiden convinced me to go back to Edinburgh with him for a week or so, if only to have a break, and he would set me up again at The Balmoral. I didn't take much convincing. I wasn't going to be like my dad. I would let this Scotsman provide me some solace in my belated grief and some time to recover from my interactions with Donald Morelli.

The plane ride from Boston to Edinburgh via Dublin went by quickly. Aiden worked on his laptop most of the flight while I slept in the adjacent seat with the help of a sleeping pill and two glasses of red wine.

A light rain was falling as we exited out of Edinburgh Airport. We hailed a taxi and Aiden dropped me off at The Balmoral before heading to his apartment.

"I have some ideas to follow up on about Alice," I said, as Aiden was helping me with my bags into the lobby.

"We'll talk tomorrow," Aiden said.

It can take a good six weeks for cracked ribs to heal, during which time you have to be careful not to move too fast, lift too much, or laugh too hard. Standing and walking were preferable to sitting or lying down. I'd been through this before when I was a teenager and a horse deposited me in front of a fence we were supposed to be leaping, so when the sun rose through my hotel window curtains at 4:40 AM, I was relieved to get on my feet, shower and go out walking.

Chapter Eighteen

There is anguish with a birthright
in flora and fauna,
like a tree's implacable search
for sustenance
when suffering from ill placed roots.
Or the confusion of a wood animal
on an asphalt road,
the reality that claims slow victims.
Do I move? Do I freeze?
If I am still and part of the night,
will I be taken down by other's
intentions?

Whether it was due to the earth heating up or present atmospheric circumstances, Edinburgh was already edging up over 25 degrees Celsius and there was not a cloud in the blue sky. As it was Sunday, the town was waking up slowly. With minimal noise from cars, buses or the tram, the birds in Princes Street Gardens were the primary ambient sound as I turned on The Mound and followed it up around North Bank Street to George IV Bridge. At this location, on the day of my eighteenth birthday, I stood at a bus stop with a young man my age who I'd met at the B&B where I was staying. He was from the Highlands and came down to Edinburgh to visit the city.

We spent several days together surreptitiously avoiding the matron of the B&B who warned us against commingling under her roof. We went to pubs, movies, parks. The most whirlwind romance I'd had in my young existence. What I remembered most was the kiss he gave me, sweeping me off my feet just before he boarded a bus to go back up north. I'd never been kissed like that before, and maybe hadn't since. I couldn't reach him after that when I got home. Common name and I probably had his address wrong. Or maybe he intentionally gave me a wrong address for reasons best known only to himself. The second in a series of missing persons in my life.

"I'll drive over and meet you in town," Aiden said, when he called my cell phone just after nine. I'd made my way down to Grassmarket. I got a cup of tea at Café Jacques and sat in the sun waiting on the patio for him. He parked and joined me at the table, ordering coffee.

"What are your brilliant ideas, my darling private detective?"

"I keep looking, Aiden, US and UK. I'm not done until I'm done."

"As far as I can see it, my mother may have come to harm by Donald Morelli along with Sheila Costa and the other desperately unfortunate women whose bodies were in his basement."

"Still no body. If he apparently had a modus operandi of dumping bodies in his cellar, why deviate from that with Alice, if he did go after her. "

"You have a point there."

"At best, we might be able to fill in some of the story from this end. One place to start, I think, is with Alice's best friend Mia Strom. It seemed odd that she was unwilling to speak with us. Maybe she knew something or heard something from Alice in those last months while Alice was with Professor Costa that she was unwilling to share. You knew Mia somewhat, right? What was your take?"

"I don't know. It was odd. I thought her to be a kind, quiet woman, the times when I met her. Her son suggested she might be having some illicit relationship. Maybe she's seeing a married man and for that reason doesn't want to socialize."

"Let's pay her a visit. Can't hurt," I said.

"Are you up to it? You're supposed to be taking a break."

"I'm good. The distraction will help."

The drive down to the Borders was healing in itself. Views of the lush countryside and the breeze from the open sunroof were calming as Aiden drove the narrow back roads along the River Tweed.

We pulled up onto the verge across from Mia Strom's terrace house, parked and went to the rear door. Aiden rang the doorbell.

Only a few seconds passed before a petite woman in her seventies, looking prim with her hair tied back in a bun and wearing a flower-patterned apron over a summer dress, opened the door. "You shouldn't be here, Aiden. But come in. Make it quick," she said hurriedly. Mia Strom looked past us and up the road briefly before following us into the hallway. She shooed us into the kitchen where we sat at a long butcher block table strewn with various cooking utensils and bowls.

"Cuppa?" she said, once we were seated. She didn't wait for an answer but turned to the stove and put a large silver kettle on the flame.

"Mia, this is my friend Mackenzie Brody. She is an investigator from the States who has been helping me look once again at my mother's disappearance. I don't mean to impose on you, but we were hoping to have a word. My sister said she spoke to you after my mother went missing, and at the time you hadn't recalled anything specific about her relationship with Professor Costa. I wondered if there is anything you can tell us in hindsight. Comments my mother might have made about him…" Aiden left off as Mia turned and raised her hands as though to stop him talking. She sat down mutely.

"I understand if you're reticent to speak about it, Mia. I know it was traumatic for you as her closest friend. But please let us fill you in on what just happened in Boston." Aiden said, then he looked over at me to continue.

"I will tell you as much as we know," I said. Mia looked at me silently but gave no further protest. "There was a colleague of Costa's, Donald Morelli, who was also a professor at the same university in

Cambridge. They worked together closely. He was recently found to have killed Professor Costa's first wife, Sheila, as well as two other women. During a confrontation with Boston Police, Morelli was killed. There has been no evidence linking him to Alice, but it seems likely that he could have been responsible for her disappearance and possibly her death as well."

Mia looked from Aiden to me, with a quizzical expression. I continued, "If you were afraid to say more about Alice and Costa's relationship due to worrying that Costa might take some retribution against you for speaking out, that danger is past. There is nothing so far pointing to Professor Costa having harmed her. Anything you can remember would be very helpful, including whether she ever mentioned Donald Morelli."

"There's nothing to worry about now that Morelli is dead," Aiden added.

Mia got up from the table and turned her back to us while she picked up the whistling kettle from the stove and took some mugs down from the shelf beside it. She turned around and placed the cups on the table and the kettle on a ceramic plate. She seemed confused, not able to decide what to do next to serve the tea. She threw up her hands and sat down.

"You are wrong lad," she said almost under her breath, closing her eyes briefly, then dabbing them with the edge of her apron.

"What do you mean?" Aiden said quietly. Tears started streaming down Mia's face. She stopped resisting them.

"The notes are still coming," she said.

Aiden stood and picked up a box of tissues from the sideboard and put them down close to her. "Please, help us to understand," Aiden said, gently prompting. "What notes? To whom?"

"The notes to your mother."

Aiden sat back in his chair and his eyes opened wide. I had the sensation of time moving like black treacle as I looked at his fingers gripping the edge of the table, knuckles white. Mia coughed as she tried to speak through her tears. "She's here, Aiden, in the Borders. She's hiding under another name."

Aiden stared at Mia and was speechless.

"Oh my God, Mia, that's incredible. That's wonderful!" I said, grabbing Aiden's arm.

Aiden cleared his throat and shook his head. I looked at his face. His eyes were wet, and his cheeks were red. All of a sudden, he exploded in a stream of words; not joyful, but angry.

"How could this be, Mia? She couldn't let us know she is alive? My wife died. My daughter needs her. I need her. She's 30 miles away and she didn't let us know that she was not dead?" Aiden stood up, unable to contain himself in a seated position any longer. "Bloody, fucking hell!"

"Please Aiden," I said, trying to calm him as Mia continued to cry silently, leaning back and forth in her chair. "Let her tell us what happened. If Alice hid from her family, she had good reason." Aiden paced, looking at the floor. He put his hands up to his face, then around his neck as though he were trying to hold his head to his body.

"I shouldn't be telling you this. It could put your family in terrible danger," Mia said.

"It's alright, Mia. You both take it easy and let's start from the beginning on what happened. You will be fine. Alice will be alright. The family will be okay, we'll make sure of it." I looked up at Aiden, who was still circling. He acknowledged me and sat down.

"I'm sorry for the outburst," he said. "This is a shock. Please tell me my mother is in good health and doing alright."

"Oh aye, she is well and always speaking of you, your sister and the grandchildren, and hoping there will be a time soon when she can reunite with you. When the emails stop coming." Aiden wiped his face with his hands, momentarily speechless.

"Sometimes she has even taken the bus up to Edinburgh or the train to Penrith and walked around near where you and Sandra live, hoping to secretly get a glimpse of one of her children or grandchildren."

"Where is she? Why is she hiding and for God sake, what are these emails?" Aiden pleaded.

"Can you start from the beginning? What caused her to leave Massachusetts?" I said, trying to install some order to the present chaos.

"I can't tell you everything," Mia said, as she was gaining her composure.

"What are you and Alice afraid of? Morelli is dead. He can't harm my mother or anyone," Aiden said.

"When did he die?" Mia asked.

"A little over a week ago," Aiden replied.

Mia put her hands in front of her on the table. "The most recent email that Alice received was two days ago. She gets them every few weeks. They warn her that if she contacts the police with any information, or if she attempts to contact Thomas Costa or if she reaches out to her family, that her children and grandchildren will be killed. She doesn't know who sends them, but she knows why."

"Okay Mia, please continue. Just tell us as much as you feel comfortable saying right now," I said, reaching across the table to touch her hands.

Mia cleared her throat and continued. "Alice was threatened by that man Donald Morelli that if she didn't leave Thomas Costa and leave the country, she would be killed. She was warned not to tell Costa or anyone about it. She was given a passport and a ticket back to Scotland under another name by someone she didn't know and told that she would have to stay away from her family and friends, or they would be harmed. She contacted me secretly when she got back. I've been visiting her these past two years. We worked out a system. We've been very careful. I helped the lass get a flat nearby and a job locally. She has a new life but is always waiting for the threats to end."

"Thank you, Mia. You've been her lifeline," Aiden said. "I need to see her. We'll help," he added.

"It's not safe. They watch her. We know they watch her."

"We'll figure out a way. No one will find out, Mia," Aiden said.

191

"I will tell her. It's up to her. Please be patient, son. She has never wanted to take any risks that could endanger you." Aiden closed his eyes, struggling. Patience wasn't his thing.

"Please let her know, Mia," I said. "We can take every precaution. We just need to see her and talk to her. There has to be a way out of this. Morelli is dead and there may be some people acting on his behalf who don't even know yet that he has died."

"I will tell her. I'll let you know. Please do not contact the police about this." Mia stood up, signaling us that she was done. As we walked to our car, Danny pulled up on a motorbike and parked, then removed his helmet. He merely nodded to us and went inside the house.

Chapter Nineteen

At the cornerstone of a weathered ruins
I stand facing the elements, fragile and burdened,
burning from the damp cold on the brae.

Needs are wrapped around me like a cloak
as a futile buffer against being alone
on the long course down the hillside.

Lost between believing and not believing
in a future, uncertainty tracks me like a wolf
across the storm-swept moor.

Aiden was agitated on the ride back to Edinburgh and driving aggressively. "Let's go to my place. Erin isn't back until tomorrow. We need to plan."

"We'll take a look at our options, Aiden. Just be calm and thankful that Alice is alive."

"Of course, I'm thankful, Mac. That goes without bloody saying."

"Would you like me to drive?" I asked. "Before you get us or someone else killed?"

Aiden shook his head and slowed down. "There have been a few times in the last two years when I've thought I saw her out of the corner of my eye, just standing on a street corner. I put it down to my wishful imagination, but it must have been her. Incredible."

We arrived at the flat, parked in the underground garage, took the elevator up to his floor and entered the flat. I went to his fridge and pulled out some cheese, setting it on a plate with crackers from the cupboard, then put on the kettle. "Food first, then planning," I said, putting it down in front of him. Aiden took a call from Erin and made arrangements to pick her up at her cousin's the following day.

"We should contact the cops first off," I said. "Whoever is threatening Alice has to be identified, and it's going to take some forensic skills."

"The problem I see with that, Mac, is that it will bring in the troops. I don't think we want to do that until my mother has agreed to see me and has been brought up to date so that she isn't frightened by the cops barging into the situation. Let's keep this to ourselves until we can figure out what's going on."

"Just because you write stories about spy capers doesn't mean you know how this should be approached. We need the experts. She may be too scared to even see you. What then?" I asked.

"How about we tail Mia, find out where my mother is and then talk to her?"

"We could have someone surveil Mia to see where she goes to find your mother, but that's no easy task in a small Scottish town. And if Mia finds out, we'll lose all trust with her."

"Physical surveillance is out, then. What about electronic surveillance?" Aiden asked.

"Even if we have some way to track her phone to find Alice, we can't go barging in. We need Mia's cooperation and Alice's. Communication, if it's an option, is always better than subterfuge. I suggest we start by you composing an email to Alice, explaining what has happened with Morelli, and have Mia forward it to her. I still think it's someone who Morelli hired to keep her in check, and they don't know yet that he is dead. Whatever crime Alice has knowledge of that precipitated this, it likely has to do with Morelli. He was the one who was going around murdering people."

"I agree. Especially since according to Mia, my mother was directed not to tell old Prof Costa that she was returning to Scotland and changing her name. This all sounds like a witness protection program. Any chance authorities in the US could have orchestrated this for some reason we haven't fathomed? Something to do with the mob, perhaps?"

"Not with the threatening notes. I can't see that happening. What's occurring is a criminal endeavor to keep your mother silent."

"I'll start composing that email," Aiden said, going across the room to grab his laptop from the desk.

"I suggest you promise that you won't do anything to jeopardize the status quo so she isn't afraid. But ask Alice to forward you the threatening

195

emails so we'll have something to start working with to understand the situation."

Aiden agonized over the wording of his email for an hour, while I caught up with the States of America news on my phone. He finished and sent it to Mia, asking her to relay it to Alice.

Aiden and I took a walk, picking up the wooded trail behind the Donaldson which led down to the Water of Leith. The stream bed was peppered with birds and ducks and the banks were muddy and green from the recent rains. One of Antony Gormley's cast iron life-size male nude figures stood in the stream, silently contemplating the woods and water. A brown and white English Springer was sloshing through the bracken along the bank, ignoring calls from his owner to return to the trail. We crossed over the wooden bridge and climbed up the log steps to the backyard of the Scottish National Gallery of Modern Art and went through the gates to the gallery's café.

Aiden kept checking his phone as we ate scones and sipped tea in the café. "Maybe if you stop looking at your email, you'll hear back," I said.

"I don't know exactly how to deal with this, finding out that my mother is here. I'm jubilant that she's alive but feeling like we lost years. And what bloody well happened? She has obviously feared for her life and ours this whole time. If I'd written this plot into a book, no one would credit it."

"If I'd found out that my brother had been alive the whole time since he disappeared, I'd be just as confused."

"I wish that you had, Mac. I'm so sorry."

Aiden's phone dinged with an email notification, and he checked it again, but it wasn't from Mia or his mother.

We walked back to the flat, retracing our steps over the Water of Leith bridge and up the hill above the stream. When we got back, Aiden's phone dinged again with an email notification. "It's from Mia," he said, as he sat down at the table to read the email. "No wait, it's from my mother! She's using Mia's email."

"Share it with me?"

Aiden started reading. "Dearest Son, I am writing this using Mia's laptop in case my email is being monitored. I am very, very sorry to have kept you in the dark, to have put you and Sandra and the grandchildren through this horrible experience. Please understand that I had no choice. I was given no choice. I was led to believe, and I truly believed, that your lives depended on it and still do. As Mia told you, I am being watched. Physical movements, perhaps phone and I don't know what else. I also would have expected, for reasons I can't reveal, that the threats would have stopped with Donald Morelli's death. But they are still coming. They know where you and Sandra live. I am occasionally sent photos of you both and your children arriving or leaving your homes and also you coming and going from your pub, to prove that they know where to find you. Mia will be providing you with copies of some of the emails I have received over the years. Meanwhile, I am safe. Please, please, until we understand that the threats are over, don't try to contact me. Don't contact the police. I am living with the hope that this will be over soon. Your loving mother."

"Christ!" Aiden said.

"Have you ever noticed any stalkers? Strange cars outside? Anyone taking photos?"

"Nothing. But there is construction and contractor traffic in the area of my flat as well as by the Black Rose, so I might not have noticed if someone blended in with them. And Sandra never mentioned seeing anything unusual around her home."

"What about Sandra? When are you going to tell her?"

"Let's go down to see her tomorrow after I pick up Erin. I need to bring Sandra in on this but not by telephone. I won't tell Erin just yet, in case it could endanger her in some crazy way."

Aiden got on the phone with his sister to arrange for us to visit her the following day, while I called Geoffrey in London, to discuss having him attempt to trace the source of the emails. I put him on notice we'd be needing his electronic forensic skills.

Aiden dropped me off back at The Balmoral after dinner. On a whim, I grabbed a taxi and had the driver drop me off on Queen's Drive at the edge of Holyrood Park, the foot of Arthur's Seat. I'd walked to the top more than once on trips to Edinburgh, the first time at dawn on a May Day, when seemingly half the townspeople were climbing up the paths to the top. Legend had it that if you washed your face in the dew as the sun rose on May 1st, you would retain your youth. It was worth doing once, although the myth didn't hold true for me for very long.

The Edinburgh sky was dusky gray, and I pulled my sweater around me against the damp breeze on the lower reaches of the hill. Several people were walking their dogs and merely nodded as they passed me. Other than the few twenty-first century humans crossing my path and the streetlights below, the view would have been nearly the same centuries ago. I'd spent time over the years walking lowland hills and Highland moors in this country; mostly alone, immersed in the mental reflection and peace that the rough beauty of Scotland's landscapes engendered. I could never get enough of it.

Aiden and I took the train down to Sandra's home in Cumbria the next day, after he'd done an early morning drive to Fife to retrieve Erin and drop her off at their flat. The train took just over an hour and a half, through rolling and wet countryside. The rain cleared by the time we got off in Penrith. Sandra met us with the car, and we drove to her residence. I noticed Aiden scope out the road, but there were no cars on the street anywhere near her house.

"You'll want to sit down for this," Aiden said, as we gathered in her living room.

Sandra looked at him with a frown. "What's wrong, Aiden? Is Erin alright?"

"Erin is fine. This is good, if shocking news. Mum is alive and well."

"What? How?" Sandra said, stuttering. As she took in the news, her eyes started to water, and her expression went from disbelief to joy. She stood up and came over to Aiden while she kept talking. "I can't believe it! Where is she? Did she have an accident? Lose her memory? Is she alright?"

Aiden stood and hugged her while she cried softly. "She's alright. We don't know the whole story yet. Far from it. She has been living in the Borders under a different name."

Sandra continued to weep while Aiden held her and attempted to explain. "She was given a fake passport and name by someone, but we don't know who they were working for. She was told to leave the States, not tell Costa, and not to contact police or anyone in her family. Mia has been staying in touch and helping her all along."

"Oh my God, Aiden. Where is she? When can we see her? When can her grandchildren see her?"

"We visited Mia yesterday, who relayed an email to her from me. Mum responded using Mia's email account. She says she is watched and that whoever is keeping tabs on her knows where you and I live, and that we'd be in danger if she contacts us or the cops. We don't know where she's living but it's near Mia somewhere in the Borders."

Aiden and Sandra sat down together on the couch, Aiden keeping an arm around her shoulders. "What can we do?" Sandra said, wiping her face with a sleeve.

"Mac and I are working on it. We'll be receiving copies from Mia of some of the threatening emails she's received, and Mac has a colleague who will do what he can to trace them. As I told you on the phone, Morelli is dead. But she has continued to get emails from someone. We'll try to get to the source. It may be that the danger has entirely passed now, but we need to move carefully."

Sandra composed herself and sat thinking for a moment. "I wonder how this person, or these people were able to keep track of what she was doing for so long? Someone has to be close to her or have access."

"Yes," I added. "It's almost beyond comprehension that someone could or would even want to have that much control over her. We assume that she has some knowledge of criminal activity by someone in Costa's sphere. She may have found out who killed Sheila Costa, and this was done to keep her quiet. The Boston PD thinks Prof Costa is not guilty of anything, but he was close to Morelli, so we can't rule out that he was somehow involved in forcing her to disappear and keep quiet."

"The police and everyone else were looking for her in America, when she was back here all the time. Incredible," Sandra said. "I'm stunned, relieved, and sick about this whole thing all at once. I can't imagine how tortuous it has been for our darling mum."

"Ach, a lot of emotions," Aiden added.

Sandra provided us with tea and lunch, then we headed back to Edinburgh on the 4:45 train. We walked across the street to the Old Waverley Hotel and took seats in their café at a bay window table with a view of the castle.

"How long can you stay?" Aiden asked after we ordered drinks.

"Nothing is too pressing back home. Another week?"

"Would you consider staying at my flat with Erin and I?" he asked hesitantly.

I didn't see that coming, but the implication was there. In my true fashion, I glossed it over. "The Balmoral is more than fine, thanks. If it's a question of the expense, I can cover it." He shifted his gaze to stare into his pint.

"No problem with the hotel charges, Mac. I just thought you might be more comfortable." The waiter came by with the food menu, and briefly acknowledged Aiden, recognizing and thanking Mr. Lindsay for his custom.

"Are you noted or notorious around here?" I said, trying to lighten the mood.

"Both."

"Meet the locals up at the Old Calton burial ground, do you?"

"Only the lucky ones," he countered, grinning.

Aiden walked me back to my hotel after dinner. Just as he was seeing me off in the lobby, his cell phone rang. It was Mia. Aiden listened to her, then turned to me.

"My mother has disappeared."

Chapter Twenty

The heart is a balance scale
measuring out how much,
how little,
increments of grace, cups of emotion.
There are delicate visions
that weaken, strengthen,
within metered phases.
Bursting full or depleted,
nearly invisible.
Gauging the reach, the receive.
Fractions of tender,
bartered caring for caring,
to find equilibrium
beyond the fragile.

Aiden motioned me over to a quiet corner and put the phone on speaker. Mia was speaking hurriedly, making her Scottish brogue harder for me to understand. "I went to see her this afternoon, and she wasn't there. I have a key, so I went inside. The wardrobe doors were open, and a few clothes were strewn around like she'd packed some and left in a fit. Her laptop was gone as well. I can't reach her by phone or text. I dinnae ken if she left on her own or was forced. Her car was not there. I phoned her work and they said she'd called in sick."

"Alright, Mia. Keep trying her. She might have become afraid and gone to a hotel. If she had time to call into her work and it looks like she packed some things, she probably wasn't taken against her will."

"This hasn't happened before," Mia said.

"Do you have some of the emails for us that she received?" Aiden asked.

"I printed some out. I was afraid to forward them to you by email. I've put them in a sealed envelope and Danny is going to drop them off to you in the morning."

"OK, I'll look for him. You have my address?" Aiden said.

"Danny said he knows where it is." Mia answered.

"Alright. Let's chat in the morning. But if you hear from her tonight, please give me a call."

"Don't mention anything to Danny, because of course he doesn't know about Alice being alive and here in the Borders. I've told him I'm sending you over some of Alice's old photos."

"He did mention the first time we stopped by that he thinks you're having an affair; that he has seen a man pick you up in a car," Aiden said.

Mia hesitated. "I've never been picked up by a man." She emphasized the word 'never,' as though insulted by the suggestion that she would be having an affair. "I always take the bus and then walk to

Alice's. I tell Danny that I'm going to the women's bingo. He makes things up, that lad."

I walked to Aiden's again first thing in the morning. Edinburgh was warm and sunny. Tourists were already starting to flock to Princes Street Gardens, which was green and lively. As I walked, I texted with Aiden who said he hadn't heard anything more from Mia as yet, in spite of having called and texted her several times, and that we'd call her again after I arrived. I walked up the drive to Aiden's flat. Aiden and Erin were having breakfast together when I arrived.

"Join us?" Aiden asked. Serving dishes were laid out with steaming scrambled eggs, smoked salmon and toast.

"Yes, thanks. Looks lovely. Who has been cooking?" Aiden pointed to Erin, who stood up from the table and went to the kitchen to get me a plate and utensils.

"Jam?" she asked me.

"By all means. What are you up to, Erin, on your school break?"

"Not much of a break," she said. "Doing online classes this summer, still trying to catch up."

"She was off from school a lot during the first term, helping take care of her mother," Aiden added.

The door buzzer rang, prompting Aiden to get up from the table. "I'll just run downstairs for a second. Delivery," he said. He returned a few minutes later with an envelope in his hand. "Some legal papers. I'll have a look at them after breakfast."

We chatted over the rest of the meal and after we finished eating, Erin cleared the table then went downstairs, excusing herself to study.

"Danny delivery?" I asked, after Erin had left.

"He doesn't say much. Scowls a bunch. Bit of a problem lad, I think."

Aiden opened the sealed envelope and took out a dozen email printouts, spreading them on the table in front of us. The full headers were shown, but the email addresses where they purportedly came from varied from one email to the next. The text varied also, some suggesting that Alice was being watched and her phone calls and emails monitored, and a few just saying 'Stay quiet. No police. No family contacts, or your children will be hurt.'

"Can you scan these to a file, and I'll send them over to Geoffrey? He can have a go at tracing the email addresses," I said. "They might be all dead ends, but if he can find anything in common with them, that might be helpful."

"Okay, I'll run them through the scanner," Aiden said.

"There's one more thing I want to have Geoffrey look into besides the emails. Professor Costa had a sister who emigrated to Australia, then eventually moved to England. Let's find out more about her and where she lives now."

I emailed the email images to Geoffrey, and asked him to run down Costa's UK sister, Paula.

We called Mia again. She picked up the phone this time, sounding distraught. "Haven't heard a thing from Alice. I'm getting fair worried, but she did call in sick again to work today, says one of her co-workers, so I think you're right that she went off by herself."

"Do you communicate to her by email usually, or phone?" Aiden said.

"We do both. I will try emailing her also in case she doesn't want to ring me."

"Whoever has been tracking her may have hacked into her email and seen our communications, and as a result put some heat on her. But there's no going back on it now, if that's the case. We need to get in touch with her and keep her safe," Aiden said.

After he hung up with Mia, I said, "Is it time to pull in your Police Scotland?"

"I don't know as they'll be of any help. She's an adult, apparently gone off on her own accord. All we have so far is some emails to show that some rank person was making threats, but no evidence that any real action was taken."

"The fact that she was supposedly dead but now isn't? Surely that would interest your CID?"

"The time will come for that," Aiden said. "Right now, I still think it would take some convincing. The cops might think I'm making the half of it up for literary purposes, not to mention they might take exception to the investigator who I brought in to help. I need to get that pub of mine opened again, then have a nice long chat with some of the local lads over a pint."

"I do think you need to bring Erin into what's happening. She's old enough to understand the need to keep things quiet right now." Aiden tapped his fingers on the table, not answering right away.

"I'm afraid that could bring her some trouble," he said finally.

"How? I think it's better she knows. She'll have your head if she finds out later that her grandmother is down the glen from here, and you didn't tell her straight away."

"Alright, I'll tell her tonight."

"Tell her now, Aiden. Trust her!"

He looked up at me with momentary indignation, then shook his shoulders and went downstairs to Erin's room without further contest. I could hear her yelling and crying a few minutes later. Somewhere between joy and angst, just like her father.

Chapter Twenty-One

In the early morning,
the grey moist light
seeps like slow wine
into the room.

In a thousand places
someone is tasting the same sunrise,
walking at the same latitude,
incredulous at the prospect
of another full cycle,
asserting a commitment to
stand and walk and reason.

There is not always agreement
from all parts
before reality subverts
the process.
Two feet hit the floor
without consensus,
and the search for balance
goes on until sundown.

The call from Alice came into Aiden's cell phone in the mid-afternoon as we were walking into his empty pub to check on how the construction had progressed in the last few days. The call wasn't from a number he recognized. She was using a pay-as-you-go burner phone. As soon as he heard her voice, he clicked on speaker, and signaled me.

"Aiden, can you hear me," Alice said.

"Mum I am so happy to hear your voice! Where are you? Are you alright?"

"I am staying at an inn for a few nights. I had to leave my flat. I'll explain. I want to meet up."

"Anywhere, you name it, and I will be there."

"Edinburgh Zoo, tomorrow noon. By the African Plains enclosure. Near the walkway along the zebra pasture where I always took the grandchildren. It's a public place. No harm could come to you there, and I can come in with the tourists."

"We'll be alright. I'm bringing my friend, Mackenzie."

Alice rang off quickly before he could say or ask anything else. Aiden pocketed his phone and spontaneously hugged and held me hard. I could feel his heart pumping.

"We're going to sort this out, Mac. I know it," he said, releasing me. "Let's have a pint to that." He went behind the bar and grabbed a couple of bottles, the draft kegs not having been replaced yet. He opened the bottles and poured glasses, then wiped the bar in front of us with a clean cloth to pick up the thin layer of construction dust. In the dim light of the bar signs, I could see his energy come back.

"Should we let Mia know she has made contact?" I asked.

Aiden picked up his phone again. Mia answered right away, and he told her that things were ok so she shouldn't worry, but he couldn't give her any details yet. Meanwhile an email came in on my phone from Geoffrey, reporting his research.

"Geoffrey says that the email addresses he has looked into so far are all defunct, as we expected. He says there's nothing sophisticated about it. Anyone could have set up the anonymous email accounts and then abandoned them. As far as Alice's computer, he needs to get into it to see if there is some malicious software installed allowing her emails and actions to be accessed. He said to let him know if we want to coordinate that between them. I told him we didn't want her computer hacked by him to accomplish that."

"What about Prof Costa's sibling here? Has he had any luck running her down?" Aiden asked. I kept reading so I could respond.

"According to Geoffrey's research, she goes by Paula Finn. She doesn't seem to work now, but he found a reference to her having done accounting work for a local manufacturing firm. One comment referencing her on a blog suggested she was fired from there. Maybe picked up some of her brother's smarts, but not enough."

"Any husband, children?" Aiden asked.

"Geoffrey says no kids. Her ex-husband was Australian. They met when she was visiting Australia. They moved to England when the husband came to work for his oil and gas firm employer here, according to an old company bio. Looks like he was running an automotive garage after that. They divorced a couple of years ago. Geoffrey sent me a photo of her that was on her social media." I showed it to Aiden. The woman in the web-posted selfie appeared tall and healthy, if a bit overweight.

"There is a definite resemblance to her sister. I hadn't compared their dates of birth, but they look about the same age. I wouldn't be surprised if they're twins. I'll have Jimmy check."

"Anything else show up?"

"Geoffrey says no criminal or even civil disputes as far as he could determine, but he hasn't been able to check the local courts. Very generic social media. Bridge club, that sort of thing. She lives in Berwick-Upon-Tweed."

"Ah, Northumberland. Close! Three miles south of the Scots border. A nice place to visit. Is that your plan?"

"We've not seen anything to indicate she's involved with any of this, but I'd like to meet her anyway. Just to see if she's as unpleasant as her sister." Aiden visibly winced at the memory of Camila Osterly.

We returned to Aiden's flat and took Erin out to dinner at the Hard Rock Café on George Street. Given her choice of restaurants, that was where she wanted to go. Against the backdrop of the restaurant's piped-in '80s rock sounds, Aiden told her we were meeting Alice tomorrow, but she would have to wait to see her until we knew what was going on with the threats. Nonetheless, I could see the excitement in Erin's countenance. She was talkative and engaged. She spoke about how she was going to take Alice to various parks and events and insist that her grandmother live close by. It was plain to see the void that Alice would be filling for this teenager on the cliff edge of adulthood.

Aiden dropped me at my hotel after dinner and said he would pick me up in the morning. Edinburgh Zoo was a stone's throw from Aiden's flat.

We arrived and parked at the Zoo at eleven, and made our way into the entrance, purposefully blending in with twenty-odd tourists who had dismounted from a holiday bus. We wandered the grounds for a while, past the giant panda enclosure and the big cats, casually checking to see if we had attracted anyone's attention or were being followed.

Just before noon, we walked up to the zebra pasture. There were scattered groups of adults with boisterous children, but no solo women to be seen. Aiden and I leaned on the fence and I took photos of the grazing zebras with my phone.

As we stood and chatted by ourselves, I noticed a slender and tall older woman ascending on the path, walking steadily toward us. She was wearing a large sunhat, sunglasses, a white blouse, and dark, tailored slacks. As she approached, Aiden turned in her direction. When she came closer, I could see tears on her cheeks under her sunglasses. They hugged briefly, Aiden wiping away his own tears with his sleeve. He took her hand and we walked further along the path to a spot off the trail where we could stop and talk privately.

"Mum, this is Mackenzie. She helped with the investigation in Boston and I brought her over to help. She is privy to everything that has happened, so you can speak freely."

Alice took my hand and looked at me with alert and kind eyes. "Thank you," she said simply.

"What caused you to leave your flat?" Aiden asked.

"I heard a motorcycle on the street yesterday morning, which isn't unusual in itself; several of the lads in the neighborhood have them. But a dead rat was left on my doorstep again. It has happened several times over the years. I became afraid that since you and I had been in touch, trouble might be brewing. I was afraid to call Mia in case my phone was being traced."

"Alice, why were you sent back from Cambridge and threatened with harm to your family if you met with them or spoke to the police? Please help us to understand the situation," I said.

She looked down at her hand that Aiden was holding. "This has to end now. I won't be kept captive to these people any longer, but you must take care until we make sure there is no danger to the family," she said.

"What is it that you know?" Aiden prodded gently.

"I found out that Donald Morelli had murdered Thomas's wife, Sheila, and Thomas was probably complicit in covering it up. Morelli bragged about it to me when he was drunk. More than once. The first time, I'd left the dining room one evening at the faculty club to visit the ladies, and on the way back he cornered me in an empty hall. He said the same thing could happen to me, that he and Thomas could make me disappear."

"Oh my God," Aiden said.

"I confronted Thomas about it. He denied knowing who killed Sheila or knowing anything about it. Thomas said he believed that Morelli was not involved in anything to do with Sheila. I didn't know what to believe, but then Morelli sought me out several times after that when Thomas wasn't around and threatened me. He said I had to leave to go back to Scotland and if I said any more to Thomas, family or the cops, he would kill me."

"How did it happen that he sent you back here?" Aiden asked.

"I suspect he or Thomas had some underworld connections, since someone produced a fake UK passport and identity for me. I didn't dare refuse to go when he threatened to seek out and harm you and Sandra and the children. He said he found out the names of the grandchildren and where you all lived."

"You did what you thought was right, Mum," Aiden said.

"I am so sorry all this happened, and that I wasn't there for you and Erin when Cheryl died. Thomas had a fine mind, but he was naïve and had a blind streak. He could have been complicit in Sheila's murder, or at least have suspected it but not done anything about it. I don't know the extent of it, but I should have recognized earlier that both of them were troubled men. Morelli could have been holding something over Thomas. Morelli and probably Thomas took away my life. They might as well have silenced me for good."

"But that didn't happen, and we are together now. We'll figure out who is behind the continued threats, and this will be over."

"I don't want whoever is watching me to know that I've broken my chains to see you. I'll go back to my flat today and carry on normally. Can you try to find out who is doing this without bringing in the police? Maybe at least we can do this quietly. Perhaps, as you said, the danger is now over, but Morelli's minions here haven't found out yet."

"I'm not sure if it would be a mistake or not at this point to bring in police. But we'll have a look at our options before we make that move," Aiden said. "Keep your pay-as-you-go phone and we'll only talk using that for now."

I stepped aside to give mother and son some privacy as they talked a while longer about how Aiden and Erin were faring since his wife died, and how Sandra and her kids were doing. Eventually we parted and went separate ways along the zoo paths.

"Alice has held up well," I said, when we returned to the car.

"She's strong. Always has been. And stubborn too, which why this went on for so long. She was determined to deal with it herself and not ask for help. Instead of potentially endangering us, she cut herself off from the family."

"If what Morelli said to Alice was true, it appears that either Costa couldn't face up to what Morelli was capable of, or Costa contributed to Sheila's death. Even when Alice disappeared, he supported Morelli without question. Morelli must have had something on Costa to keep him in check like that," I said.

"Too much bloody control going on here."

"And that from someone who likes to be the one in control," I added. Aiden glanced over at me but didn't take the bait.

Geoffrey called while we were driving back. I picked up the call on my cell and put it on speaker so Aiden could listen in.

"I'm in the car with Aiden. What's up?"

"I've been able to trace a few of the threatening emails. They originated from a computer in a public library in Massachusetts."

"That's interesting, and not entirely surprising. Were you able to pinpoint what town?"

"Yes, Quincy. Mean anything to you?"

"It's a Costa and Morelli hotbed. Camila Osterly, Thomas Costa's sister, lives there. Good chance it was her. We know she was close with Morelli. And when Aiden and I went to see her last week, she was threatening me with consequences if I contacted her brother again. What were the dates on those emails from Quincy Library; before or after Morelli died?"

"A couple scattered over the last year and one last Wednesday."

"The most recent one would have been after Morelli died and after Aiden and I saw her. Camila knew then that he was dead, and it appears she still sent Alice a threatening email. Was it possible all of the emails were coming from Camila, but only a couple were traceable?"

"Entirely possible she was the source of all of the threats. She might have just slipped up on a few emails by not deleting those accounts," Geoffrey said.

"But even if it was her sending the emails, she still has to have boots on the ground here, since dead rodents have been left on Alice's doorstep," I said.

"Right. She could be hiring someone locally. Not hard to do if you've got even a small bit of internet savvy."

"Thanks, Geoffrey. I'll keep you posted."

"Stay out of trouble, Mac. If you can." I hung up and looked at Aiden. He was biting his lower lip while driving.

"Fuck these people," he said.

"I'm putting Jimmy on this to see if he can find out if Camila frequents the Quincy Library computer room." I texted Jimmy the particulars as we pulled in and parked at Aiden's flat, and asked him to see what he could find out and get back to me.

As we went up the elevator from the garage, I was anticipating having a glass of wine with Aiden, then returning to my hotel for a quiet evening. It was anything but. Erin was nowhere to be found.

Chapter Twenty-Two

There is a quiet, broad solo
evolving from minor cosmic scales
to dissonant chords.
Inconsonant, conflicting powers,
drifting into God-like harmonic refrains.
Back and forth,
following some unchartered melodic pattern.
Unmindful of the beat of humankind,
of the soothing touches,
the harsh pain,
the giving of freedoms,
or wearing of bonds.

"She was going to stay home today and study," Aiden said, after we went into the flat and Erin was not in evidence. He tried to reach her by text and then by calling, with no response. The phone call went to her voice mail and the text was not returned.

"Check her room to see if her cell and bag are still there? Maybe she went out for a walk without either." Aiden went downstairs and came back empty handed.

"No phone, no bag. Wherever she has gone, those are with her. I'll give it awhile to see if she gets back. She might not have enough signal where she is right now. Mobile signal can be spotty in town."

Aiden pulled out some snacks, and we remained in the kitchen while he kept checking his phone. "I'll call Sharon, her best friend, to see if she knows Erin's whereabouts." Sharon answered his call but said she hadn't seen or heard from Erin in a couple of days. Aiden was patient for exactly two hours, calling and texting Erin every fifteen minutes with no response.

"It's been too long," he said. "This is not like her. She is good at responding usually."

"Are there cameras outside the building here?"

"The office has security cameras in the lobby and outside on the drive. I'll call the security office and ask them to check for her. I know the guys who rotate through the schedule. They'll do it for me without any hassle." Aiden got on the phone again and spoke to the duty person in the office, who said he'd go back over the video from the late morning when we left until the time we arrived back in the afternoon. A few minutes later he called back and asked Aiden to come down to the office.

The man who answered when we went down to the property office filled the doorway as he unlocked it and motioned us in. "Mac, meet Big Jon," Aiden said. Consistent with his name, Jon was bulging out of his dark blue uniform shirt that sported a private security logo over his heart. In spite of his heft, Jon adroitly positioned himself on a small stool at a desk with several computer screens.

"Look here, there's a car pulling up beside her." He switched from still image to scrolling video which was time coded just after 1:00 PM. Erin was leaning down to respond to a driver in the car, who had the passenger side window rolled down. She then opened the front passenger door and got inside. The car pulled away, but the side angle of the camera did not allow for a view of the plates. It was impossible to see the driver's face, or whether there were any passengers in the back seat.

"Do you recognize the vehicle, Mr. Lindsay? Could it be a friend of hers? A white, recent model Volkswagen. She seems to get into the car quite willingly, as though it's someone she knows."

"No, I don't, but let me make a couple of calls to her friends and also try calling Erin again. Thanks very much for your help. If she doesn't turn up soon, I'll call the police and they'll need that footage."

Big Jon saw us to the door, and we went back up to the flat. Aiden immediately tried calling Erin again, with no response. A minute later, Alice called. Aiden put her on speaker. Her voice was high pitched, and she spoke quickly.

"They've taken Erin. I just had an email. Oh God, Aiden! I've caused this."

"Slow down Mum. Read me the email," Aiden said, incredibly calmly for someone whose daughter was in danger, but I could see beads of sweat on his face.

"It says, 'Regretfully you have been in touch with your family. We have invited your grandchild to join us this afternoon to show you that we are serious about you not sharing information with family, friends or the police. You must now impress upon your son and daughter that this is a personal matter between us, and that all will be well if we keep it that way. If the police are brought in, harm will result. We have many resources here and do not want to have to use them. We will be back in touch soon.'"

"I want you to respond to the email. Say that you agree, and that you want to know where Erin is right now, so that her father can pick her up immediately. If she is unharmed, we agree to keeping this matter private."

"Alright, I'm typing it right now. Sending."

"Did it go through?" I asked. "I hope that email address is not already defunct."

"Yes, apparently it went through. It didn't bounce back," Alice said. "Oh, I see there's a response. It just says, 'We'll be in touch soon."

"Alright, Mum, just stay put. Call me immediately if you receive any more communication. I'll let you know what we're doing on this end."

"Aiden, there's one more thing," she said.

"Yes?"

"When I got back to the house this afternoon, I saw a motorcycle in front of the flat. I recognized the driver when he took off his helmet. It was Danny, Mia's son. He took off before I could signal him. Maybe he has a friend in the neighborhood. I don't know."

"Danny!" I said, when Aiden had hung up. "I think he's a conduit here. It makes sense that he might have been the one feeding information to someone as to Alice's movements. And probably dropping off the dead rats. All along he could have been undermining Mia by reporting on Alice."

"Danny said he knew who I was when we saw him, and Mia did say Danny knew where I lived, which surprised me because I've never invited him over here. He will know who is behind this, where they are, and probably where they have Erin. Let's get in the car. We're going to Mia's," Aiden said. We raced down to the garage and took off toward Galashiels.

"This is a hostage situation, Aiden. It's time to bring in the cops. We aren't equipped to handle this," I said as he drove.

"I've got this, Mac."

"No, you haven't got this. You need an experienced negotiator to make sure Erin isn't hurt. You're not James fucking Bond. A wrong move could make this go badly. This is a law enforcement specialty, not yours or mine."

"I want to give Danny a chance to work with us. I don't want him arrested and questioned while Erin is being held somewhere. If he won't cooperate, that's what will have to happen. We'll bring in the cops.

"You're taking a big chance here," I said. "How about calling them right now?"

"It might surprise you that I do know something about hostage negotiations."

I looked over at Aiden. He wasn't smiling. "Yeah, I'm sure you've read about it somewhere," I said.

Aiden pulled the car over and grabbed his phone. He pulled up a number for the Edinburgh Divisional Headquarters of Police Scotland from his contacts and dialed.

When the call was answered, Aiden said, "My name is Aiden Lindsay, I live in Edinburgh, and I need immediate police assistance." He gave a short explanation, including that he'd recently found out that his mother, who had gone missing in the States two years ago, was living in the Borders under a false name after she was forced to leave the States due to threats from a man who turned out to be a serial killer. The Constable on the other end may or may not have believed the story but asked for more details.

Aiden said, "This has all happened quite quickly here, and I was afraid to contact the police initially. But my fourteen-year-old daughter, Erin, has been kidnapped by someone involved in this. She got into a car with someone this afternoon, according to CCTV at my flat in West Coates, and hasn't been heard from since. Then my mother received an email a little while ago saying they have her. Whoever 'they' are. I'm headed right now to the home in Galashiels of her best friend, Mia Strom, who has been her ongoing contact here. We have reason to believe that her son may be collaborating with the perpetrators and might know where Erin has been taken."

Aiden was directed to provide them with Mia's address and told that he would be met there by someone from the local Borders station.

Once Aiden pulled back out on the road and continued driving, I texted Geoffrey to drive north towards the Borders from where he'd been working in Berwick-Upon-Tweed. I shared my location with him on the mobile phone so he could find us wherever we ended up. I didn't tell Aiden. This one was on me.

When we pulled onto the verge across from Mia's, Danny's motorbike was parked in front. We pushed the doorbell, and Mia answered.

"What is happening, Aiden?" She asked.

"Mum is safe. She's back at her flat. She became fearful when another dead rodent was left on her doorstep."

"Oh, thanks goodness she's alright!" Mia said.

"Mia," I said, "Alice saw Danny on her street this morning, on his bike. Do you know if he has any friends over that way, or why he might have been there?"

"No, I don't. He doesn't have a lot of friends, really. At least none that I know of over that way."

"We'd like to speak with him," Aiden said. "Erin is now missing, and it seems she's being held by the same people who have been threatening my mother. If Danny knows or has seen anything, that could help." Mia immediately left the room and went up the stairs calling his name. A few moments later, they came back down the stairs together.

"Danny, I expect you know where my mother is staying?" Aiden asked. Danny sat on a kitchen stool and squirmed, his eyes moving around the kitchen. "Please talk to us. This is a serious matter. My mother

225

has been continually threatened, and now my daughter has been taken. Her life may be in danger."

Danny continued to move his feet around under his stool and look anywhere but at Aiden. "Don't know nothin'," he said, half under his breath.

"Why were you by her house this morning? Has someone been sending you to watch her? You can tell us. I understand if you were pressured to do that. If you help us, it will all be ok," Aiden added. "You and Erin were always childhood friends. Please, her life may depend on it."

"I don't know who it's for."

"Who what was for?" I asked.

"They just asked me to go over there sometimes, and to take a few pictures at your house and your sister's. Didn't see no harm in it. Nobody was hurting anyone, just trying to keep track of things."

"Danny, did you know who this person was who was directing you?"

"Never met them. Only emails, and they gave me some money once. It was so I could buy my new motorbike. The old one was falling apart. My ma didn't have the money and I couldn't find work."

"Danny! I can't believe you would have done such a thing. This is my friend. You did this behind my back. How could you even…" Mia was standing by the sink. The color drained from her face as she spoke.

"Didn't seem like no big deal."

Mia started crying and left the room, holding her hand up in front of her mouth. I could hear her gasping for breath between sobs in the next room.

"If you're found aiding and abetting the threats to my mother, and the kidnapping of Erin, you won't have need for a motorbike. You'll be incarcerated for a bloody long time," Aiden said angrily.

"Danny, do you have any idea where this person would have taken Erin?" I asked.

"Nope."

"Did they have you pick up the money from them?" I asked.

"Yeah. When I picked up the cash for the new bike, it was a garage in Duns."

"Who met you?" I asked.

"A man. Just seemed to work at the garage. Handed me an envelope. We didn't talk."

"How long ago was that?" I asked.

"Last year," Danny said.

"Do you remember the address?" Aiden said.

"Nope, but I know how to find it. It's off the main road."

"Come with us," Aiden said, taking Danny's arm as Mia came back in the kitchen. "Mia, wait here until the police arrive and fill them in, then go over to Alice's and stay with her. Call me if mother hears anything more and call the police if you see anyone approaching her flat. I'll text you where we end up in Duns so the police can meet us there." Mia nodded silently, in utter shock at her son's complicity.

During the forty-five-minute drive, Danny barely spoke. Other than giving occasional directions, he stayed morosely quiet in the back seat.

When we pulled up to the garage in Duns where Danny directed us, Aiden parked across the street. It was a stand-alone commercial building with three garage bay entrances, which were all shut. Graffiti was sketched on the bay doors, and a 'To Let' sign was stuck on the verge out front. There was no sign of activity save one car parked in the drive. It was a white Volkswagen. Aiden punched the address into a text to Mia and opened the car door.

"Stay here, Danny. Don't move a fucking muscle." Aiden said as he got out. I followed, signaling that I would go around to check the back of the building, while he went to the front entrance.

Chapter Twenty-Three

Behind me,
I've been seeing shadows.
Ahead, a stomach clutching fear.
Emotions are coming to me
like part of the earth, betrayed.

The future is an unknown dream
I'll be surprised to have survived.

I walked quickly along the side of the building over the broken concrete and around the back of the garage. A gravel driveway wound around the rear of the building and back up to the road. There were several rusted steel drums stacked against the concrete wall beside an old trash bin that was overflowing with pieces of twisted metal and rags. There were a few windows high up on the outer wall and one door, which was slightly ajar. I pushed the door open slowly. I couldn't see anyone or hear any voices. I opened the door further and stepped inside.

The rear door accessed the bay area, which was strewn with old car parts and discarded and broken tools. The light from the windows was enough to illuminate the garage and show a couple of separate rooms, which I assumed to be offices, at the opposite end from where I entered. One room had a glass window looking out over the bays. I saw movement inside the office but wasn't able to make out details from across the garage, so I worked my way across the room along the back wall, stepping over the debris.

I could see two entrances to the office, one just inside the garage leading to the outside front of the building, and another in the rear corner of the garage with a small window on the door. As I came closer to the door at the back, I could hear the murmur of voices. Through the murky glass I saw Aiden standing just inside the office, gesturing to someone who was standing with their back to the glass.

I walked closer to the rear office door, where I could see Aiden more clearly. It was a woman he was gesturing to. She was not much shorter than Aiden, appeared older and had mid length, brown hair, but I couldn't see enough of her face to try and identify her. There was a chair to her right with Erin sitting in it, facing Aiden. I could see that Erin's hands were secured somehow behind her back, and there was tape around her middle, tying her to the chair. The woman had a small gun in her right hand. I silently turned the doorknob and cracked open the door, so I could hear their conversation.

"If you release Erin to me now, we'll call it a draw," Aiden said. "We'll forget this happened and you can go about your life. There will be no police…"

The woman raised her shrill voice, interrupting Aiden. "You people have interfered. Alice was compliant. She left Thomas and kept her mouth shut, even though none of what she thought she knew was true. She was poison."

"What happened that upset you?" Aiden asked.

"She was going to destroy Thomas and Donald and had to be stopped. She accused Donald of murdering Thomas's wife and Thomas of helping. Alice is poison. Your daughter is poison," the woman ranted, waiving the small semi-automatic pistol in the air.

Overhearing her accusations, coupled with recalling the photo of her that Geoffrey had sent, it became clear to me who Aiden was facing. This was Paula Finn, Thomas Costa's other sister.

"There is no reason for this," Aiden continued, calmly. "We will put it behind us. You will never hear from us or Alice."

"My sister knew there was going to be trouble. We had it under control. It won't stop now."

Paula stepped toward Erin, who started crying and squirming, trying to shake off the chair she was tied to. Paula waived the gun at Erin's head, yelling at Aiden. "Go and tell Alice her granddaughter paid."

I pushed open the door with a hard shove and lunged toward Paula. I pulled her away from Erin. As we struggled, I grabbed her weapon arm and we both fell to the floor.

The advantage I had in fitness was up against her bulk as I moved to get out from under her and get my right hand on the butt of the weapon. I tried to fend her off as she scrambled with both of her hands to get a proper grip on the gun and force it down toward my chest. In the struggle, she got off one shot that went wild. It was enough to prove to me that the pistol was actually loaded, and she'd known enough to chamber the first round. She finally succeeded in pointing the weapon and getting a finger on the trigger. I stopped resisting and lay still. No one in the room moved.

"Get up," she shouted, moving off of me and standing up, while she kept the gun pointed in my direction. It was a small black pistol that resembled an old .22 caliber Manurhin that I'd used at the range once. That one had a habit of jamming. You never knew if the shot was going to go off or not when you pulled the trigger. It looked like James Bond's Walther PPK because they were made in the same French factory post-war. The fact that it was only .22 caliber didn't mean it was any less lethal. A small caliber bullet could do as much damage as a larger one. It had the potential to ricochet around inside your body, tearing up organs, rather than creating a clean hole that could maybe be patched up if you didn't bleed out first.

I got up off the floor slowly, scoping out everything in the room; her position, my position, whether Aiden or Geoffrey, who had just arrived and was standing behind him, could intervene. The woman was unpredictable, certainly unbalanced. She might fire or she might not. The old pistol she held, that maybe she'd found in her Australian ex-husband's closet, might jam or not.

"Go through there," She shouted at me, pointing the gun that she now held with both hands at a door behind me that led to another small office.

I opened the door and went through into a semi-dark room that was illuminated only by a dirty skylight. The room held a couple of metal desks, chairs, and file cabinets, along with scattered paper debris on the floor. The air was dank from lack of ventilation.

I walked ahead of her as she followed me closely into the room. As I felt the gun barrel being pressed against my back, I was calculating my chances of disarming her. Once we got into that room, she had few choices. She was cornered as well as I was, and only one of us was likely to survive. I figured it would be over quickly or turn into an extended hostage situation. I wasn't having any of it.

After we crossed the threshold where I figured she couldn't hit anyone else with a wayward bullet, I spun on my heels and raked my arm across her face with the full force of my body. She got off a shot that went toward the ceiling, but she was off balance and tumbled to the floor. She went down with the gun still in her hand. I was on her in a second. I took advantage of her awkward fall to dive on her prone figure and grab her weapon hand and smash it against the cement. The gun went skittering across the floor. In that same second, Aiden and Geoffrey came bursting into the room and were both on top of her, pinning her to the floor while I rolled off of her and stood up.

She screamed but was overpowered. While they held her down, I grabbed the roll of gaffer tape from the next room that she'd used to tie up Erin, handed it to Aiden and they began wrapping her hands and feet to immobilize her. Aiden ripped another piece off the roll and stuck it over her mouth to stop the noise coming from it.

I left Aiden and Geoffrey to finish securing Paula Finn, and went to Erin, who was crying quietly, still strapped to the chair. I started pulling the tape off that held her. When I finished and she could stand, I hugged her while her father and Geoffrey continued to wrap rounds of tape over Paula's flailing legs.

"Christ, you're bleeding, Erin," I said, pulling away to see where the blood was emanating from. She had a slight graze on her right shoulder, apparently from the first shot that had gone wild. It was oozing, but slowly. I pulled some tissues from my pocket and pressed them against it to stem the bleeding.

The sound of an approaching siren outside was audible. "We can hand this nightmare over to them," Aiden said. Geoffrey hurried out the front door to meet the cops and let them know the situation was under control and they could enter the building without endangering anyone.

Moments later two of Police Scotland's finest from the local Duns station made their way into the room. They'd been requested to respond by the Borders division officer who appeared at Mia's house after we left. The constables asked us all to stay where we were while they figured out what had happened and to whom.

A few minutes later, a detective inspector from the Duns Police Station appeared. A big man, matching Aiden's height, he was plain-clothed, with brown slacks and a light tan jacket over a white shirt. Rather than regular shoes, he wore a pair of work boots that had seen some mud. He introduced himself as DI Roberts, then without saying anything, surveyed the scene. Meanwhile one of the uniforms was putting the gun in an evidence bag.

"I can hardly feel it. Just burns a little bit," Erin said, as Aiden came over to look at her shoulder.

Aiden turned to Roberts. "She won't need an ambulance, but we should get her to hospital to check that out and her condition generally," Aiden said. "I'd like my friend here, Mackenzie, to take her to urgent care in Duns to be looked at."

"And you are?" Roberts asked, directing his question at me.

"This is Mackenzie Brody. She's family friend visiting me from the States," Aiden interjected. I left it at that, figuring there would be time later to provide more of an explanation. I assumed Aiden was calculating that reporting my occupation and relationship to the investigation right now would likely have made for a longer evening.

"Give the constable your passport and contact details, then you can go." Roberts said.

"My bag is in Aiden's car, along with Danny," I said.

"He'll need to speak to these officers," Aiden added. Geoffrey went outside to the car, brought Danny in and handed me my bag. I pulled out my passport and gave it to the officer, who took a photo of it with a mobile phone. "I'm at The Balmoral," I said. The officer handed me back my passport. Geoffrey walked us out to the street to Aiden's car and I headed with Erin to the local hospital.

Meanwhile Aiden, Geoffrey and Danny remained behind to explain to the police the events that led to having a large duct taped woman muttering incoherently on the floor.

Chapter Twenty-Four

I didn't intend to find such unrest,
when mining for portions of myself
that denied exposure
to touch and air.

I know more than before about losing,
less about standing still,
more about moving.

What I thought I knew keeps changing.
But if I have nothing else,
I've had much,
and I won't be careful this gentle evening.

While I waited at the hospital for Erin to be tended to, Jimmy called my mobile. I filled him in on current events, then asked for his update.

"I called the Quincy library. It didn't take much effort to find out that Camila Osterly volunteers there a couple of days per week, helping young school kids with the library computers," Jimmy said. "Also, I checked birth dates and Camila and Paula are twins."

"They both had motive and opportunity for sending Alice nasty emails," I said. "Can you give Detective Connor a call and relay that info? They can take it from there."

"Will do, Mac. Glad you're all okay. See you when you're back here," Jimmy said, ringing off.

After the initial police interviews were done and Paula Finn had been hauled off in a patrol car, Aiden, Alice and Geoffrey met Erin and I at the community hospital in Duns.

Erin was patched up at the Duns hospital to the tune of just a few stitches, and amazingly, she was clear-headed and showing no signs of shock from her experience. "Luckily Paula Finn was not very adept with a pistol," I said, as we gathered in the lobby.

"Yes, could have been worse by a stretch," Aiden said. He was holding Erin's hand and looking at her. The color had returned to her face, and she seemed none the worse for having been kidnapped by a ghost from her grandmother's past. Alice, for her part, had one arm around Erin's waist.

"Mia dropped my mother off to us at the garage in Duns for an initial chat with the police, and then she hauled Danny home until he's called in for further questioning by the coppers. He's going down for some discipline by the courts," Aiden said.

"How are you feeling, Erin?" Alice asked.

"I'm good, thank you. All of you," Erin said shyly. "I'm so sorry I accepted a ride with that woman. She said she knew you, and Mia and Danny. I thought she was a family friend. She offered to drop me off at the bus stop. Seemed nice. After I got in the car, she pulled out that gun and told me to sit still and hand over my phone. Then she drove to the garage and made me sit there all taped up for a couple hours. She went on about how my grandmother was a danger to her brother. She yelled at me to shut up every time I tried to talk to her."

"Don't worry Erin. None of this was your fault. She would have found some way to cause harm in any case," Aiden said.

"You came fast. I knew you would," Erin said. Aiden gave her a hug, then turned to me. "You're okay Mac?"

"Good, thanks, but I'll need some food and drink. I expect I speak for all of us on that score."

After we said our goodbyes to Geoffrey, the four of us got in Aiden's car and headed to Edinburgh. Aiden called ahead to his sister to arrange for Sandy and her husband to meet us.

After an emotional reunion amongst the family members upon arrival, Sandy began heating up some food that she'd brought while the rest of the family gathered around Aiden's kitchen table. Aiden passed around the wine bottle. "Have a glass, you've earned it," Aiden said, pouring a French white for Erin.

"Some wine, Mac?" Aiden asked, motioning to an empty glass.

"Thanks, but I'll head back to my hotel. Let all of you catch up." Aiden looked at me, then poured wine into the crystal wine glass on the table.

"Please stay?" Aiden asked. I wasn't entirely comfortable being an intruder in their family reunion and Aiden sensed it. I wasn't too comfortable with him reading my mind either.

"You're part of this crazy Clan Lindsay now, Mac. Like it or not. Get used to it," he said. I sat down at the table. I had to admit that I was feeling some deep affection for this group. It was already well beyond a client relationship.

"Grandma, how did they keep you hidden for so long?" Erin asked, after everyone was settled in.

"I was constantly threatened, Erin. I followed their instructions to protect the family."

"Considering how unhinged Paula Finn is, not to mention the assistance she was getting from Costa's other sister, I think you did right, Mum," Aiden said.

"Thank you, Mackenzie, for guiding Aiden down this path to find me, and for keeping Erin safe," Alice said.

"The police will be talking to all of us again in the next day or so to get the full account." Aiden said. "They will also talk with Boston Police who will deal with Thomas Costa and Camila Osterly. They'll get their comeuppance, however they were involved," he added.

"I'll be interested in finding out what, if any, involvement Thomas had in all of this," Alice said. "It seemed all so unlike him. We had our arguments. He was set in his ways and more difficult to live with than I'd anticipated. But he was not unkind to me and we got along well for the most part. I must say, though, his sister, Camila, never liked me and she was putting pressure on Thomas to end our relationship."

"Which is probably why Costa was disparaging of you when I interviewed him," I said. "He was taking a cue from his sisters, who had their own reasons for wanting to protect him. Morelli undoubtedly never admitted to Camila that he told you himself that he killed Sheila Costa. But, however it was that Morelli told the sisters you came by that information, they all wanted you stopped in your tracks before you went public with it."

"Donald Morelli always seemed to be around Thomas. They were close. He was like part of the family, I know that," Alice said.

"Somewhat perversely, it might have been because the sisters were keeping track of you that you didn't end up being one of Morelli's basement victims before you could leave Cambridge. He was a serial killer, but he couldn't make you vanish without them knowing," I said.

After we had dinner, Aiden drove me back to my hotel. He pulled up in front of The Balmoral, then turned to look at me for a long moment.

"You'll want to stay a few more days until the police inquiries are finished. And you're not fit to travel yet in any case. We'll not discharge you from Scotland until you have fully mended. If you agree, of course."

I laughed. The Scotsman seemed to be mitigating his impulse to control my schedule. "I'll book a flight to go home next week. I need some time in the marina, on the water, after all this."

"Ah yes, boat life. I should like to visit you onboard."

"You'll be welcome, of course. Just make sure your family stays intact while you're away."

"I'll put my mother in charge of the teenager while I'm away. She'll regret the day she came back to us."

We got out of the car and Aiden walked me up to my room. As he opened the door for me, I noticed that there was no longer a wedding ring on his left hand.

"Get the Black Rose up and running again and I'll come back here to visit. Meanwhile, I'll have a chance to read one of your books. Then while I'm lounging on my yacht recovering from having met you, maybe I can work out which intelligence service you had affiliations with."

"Good luck with that, darling." Aiden put his arms around my neck and leaned down, his head against mine. I felt his breath on my face. "Just come back, Mackenzie," he said.

I thought he was going to kiss me. He hesitated, touched my cheek and pushed the bangs out of my eyes. I grabbed him around his waist, pulled him toward me and kissed him hard on the mouth. Like the unforgettable kiss I had on a street corner in Edinburgh the day I turned 18. After a time, he stepped back into the hallway, smiling. "Lunch at my place tomorrow with the Lindsays, Mac. But call me if you can't sleep tonight."

Chapter Twenty-Five

I am soaring out of my skin,
a hawk in flight
in a quiet yellow dusk.
A feather dropped
and remembered
with affection,
not with a sad heart.

A hawk not owned or coupled,
passing through
on the jet stream.
Remember me as I was
in my finest flight.
I am here as love only.

A week later I flew to Boston via London, meeting Jimmy at Logan Airport and settling in at Morgan's for a few days. I felt pretty well recovered, the residual pain from cracked ribs having mostly subsided.

Kenneth's remains had been released by the coroner to the mortuary, so Morgan and I made a plan for a small memorial gathering for him at her place with the few relatives I still had in the area. I wouldn't try to bring my father to the reception at Morgan's, but Jimmy said he would drive out to Topsfield to pick him up and bring him to the cemetery for the graveside honors.

I drove into the city on my first full day there to see Detective Connor. He met me at the PD reception desk and took me back to his office. I sat across from him at his cluttered desk. He moved some files aside out of his way so he could rest his elbows on the surface. Some exhaustion was showing around the edges of his usually alert demeanor.

"Welcome back to Boston. It sounds like you had some adventures in Scotland."

"It has been a wild ride, Detective. Where does it stand with Costa?"

"We brought Costa in for an interview. He did not admit to knowing that Morelli killed his first wife. Whether Costa really knew and was involved in covering up her murder or whether Morelli used that as a tactic to frighten Alice Lindsay, we don't know. With Morelli dead, it's going to be hard to prove. Costa may have to keep that one on his conscience."

"What about Alice's de facto kidnapping?"

"Costa also stood his ground on that. Said he did not participate in sending Alice Lindsay back to the UK under another name and force her to keep quiet. It looks like his sister, likely both sisters, orchestrated that with Morelli and they kept it going after he was killed."

"Both Camila and Paula, the horrible twins, probably had a hand in all along," I said.

"Yes, we will get some traction on that with the help of the initial research you did to link Camila to the emails sent from the Quincy Library. We're pulling her in for questioning and coordinating with the police in the UK. She'll go down with Paula Finn for involvement with Alice's forced move and confinement, once we verify her involvement. Subpoenas for her phone records and computer, as well as the library computers, are in process."

"I don't see how Costa could not have known about Sheila's murder. Morelli had a hold over Costa. I doubt that Costa's and Morelli's shared academic improprieties would have given Morelli enough of a grip on Costa to cover up the murder of his wife, if that's what went down. But Morelli must have been privy to the fact that back in the day, Costa was cooking the books for his father's business."

"You're likely right. Even more than that. Morelli was Costa's half-brother."

"Ah, blood ties. The thickest. Father, son, twin sisters, half-brother. A crime syndicate of one family. Morelli lied to my face that he knew the old man."

"DNA samples we took from both of them told that story, and when we confronted Costa with it, he said he and his sisters and Morelli knew they were all related, but that knowledge was kept within the family to protect their father. I'll let you know if we turn up anything implicating Costa."

"Thanks," I said, taking my leave from his office. This time I didn't even pretend to promise I'd let things go as they were. I still had a nagging sensation that there was a knot left untied.

Aiden phoned me as I was driving back to Morgan's from the police station.

"Something you'll be interested to hear," Aiden said, after I'd updated him on the meeting with Connor.

"When Danny was brought into the police station for an interview about his interactions with Paula Finn, he was identified as the chap who had been driving around Edinburgh on his motorbike periodically for some bag snatching. He admitted to it and said it was when he came up to town to take the photos of my whereabouts that he supplied to Paula. The night he saw you walk up to Calton Hill, he'd been by the Black Rose to see if I was there. He thought you were a tourist and that you'd be an easy target."

"I'm glad to know it wasn't a local perpetrator. Danny graduated from spying on Mia, Alice and you to rat delivery and then petty theft in Edinburgh. Poor Mia," I said.

"I've spoken to her since he was arrested. She's just as glad to see him learn a lesson before his penchant for criminal behavior escalates."

"Yes, I hope he can turn around."

"I wish I was there to come to your brother's service. But need some time here with my mother to get her settled in a flat near us. She and Erin are both in great spirits. Thank you, darling."

"I'm so happy to hear that. I'll be seeing you, Aiden." I hung up before I could miss him more.

Halfway back to Morgan's, I made a U-turn and drove into Cambridge. I parked behind the square, then wandered into Harvard Yard where summer students were milling around, some taking in the sunshine on the wide steps of the Harry Elkins Widener Library. Harry, Harvard alumnus, died along with his father when the RMS Titanic foundered in 1912. His mother survived the sinking, and several years later, she dedicated the memorial library in his honor. It was a good thing to honor the past. I wasn't done with it.

I walked a few streets over to Professor Thomas Costa's house and rang the bell. It crossed my mind that neither Jimmy nor Aiden would be amused that I was doing this alone. I didn't care.

Costa answered the door almost immediately. I wasn't quite ready for his prompt appearance, or his opening the screen door and aggressively stepping out onto the patio in my face. I preferred the somewhat soporific Costa I'd encountered on my prior visit. I took two steps back.

"Professor, I expect you remember me from a couple of weeks ago when I stopped by?"

"I don't have anything to add. I spoke with the police. I'm glad to hear Alice Lindsay has been found. That's the end of it."

"Yes, I spoke with the Detective myself this morning. I understand you said you had no knowledge of Alice's forced trip home and confinement back in the UK. I wanted to talk to you about someone else."

Costa didn't move. He stood where he was and made no motion to sit down in his corner rocking chair to relax and have a nice chat.

"About whom?"

"Sheila."

"What about Sheila?"

"Donald Morelli. You two were close. You were half-brothers. You knew each other's secrets. You'd seen his behavior toward women. I can't fathom that you did not know or at least deeply suspect him of killing her and others. And you let it go." I paused, searching for other words, and failing. "You let it go. You let it happen."

Costa closed his eyes for a moment. I waited. That's all I could do.

He finally spoke, pronouncing his words slowly and succinctly. "Whether I knew or whether I did not know, that changes nothing."

It wasn't the response I was anticipating, but I don't know what I was expecting to hear or accomplish.

"Live with it," I said. I turned on my heels and walked down his front steps to the street.

The cemetery which held my mother's grave was at the edge of a lake in Wakefield, Massachusetts, twenty minutes north of the city of Boston. Kenneth's plot was next to my mother's, near a grove of trees at the shoreline. The grass was muddy from recent rains, and the July heat was just short of oppressive. Morgan, Jen and I went together in one car. A few cousins and nephews who had joined us at Morgan's for a memorial gathering beforehand arrived in separate cars, and Jimmy brought my father.

As we were walking across the lawn to the grave site, I saw that my ex-husband was there, standing by the casket in his US Air Force dress blues. I caught my breath at the sight of him, remembering how I'd asked him to wear that same jacket for our wedding. I went over to him and gave him a hug.

"I didn't know you were coming."

"Got the details from Morgan. I asked her not to tell you in case I couldn't make it. I was able to switch flights at the last minute."

"Thanks for being here, Peter."

"I know how much this means to you, that Kenneth's story is solved."

"Join us tonight for dinner at Morgan's?"

"I'd like to, but I'm in the driver's seat at 1800 hours back to LA."

"My dad is here. He probably won't remember you but say hello after the ceremony anyways."

"Will do."

Jimmy walked my father slowly over to where we gathered. I gave my father a kiss on the cheek and stood aside with him, holding his arm while Kenneth's small wooden casket was lowered into the ground by the cemetery staff. Jimmy read an Irish blessing and a poem I'd written that I didn't feel capable of reading aloud myself, then he threw a handful of earth on top of the casket.

I stayed with my father, who was silent but seemed somehow to know. When our improvised lay service was finished, Peter came over to speak with him briefly. My father smiled when his former son-in-law expressed his condolences but showed little recognition. Peter waved goodbye to me and went to his car.

Jimmy and I walked my father back to Jimmy's car which was parked along the cemetery road. I hugged my dad by the open passenger door. He didn't resist, and I could feel him, just lightly, touch my back.

"Dad, you still have a daughter. That would be me. I will come to see you again soon. I love you."

"We found him, didn't we?" he said.

"Yes, we found Kenneth."

I helped my father get in the passenger seat and closed the door, then Jimmy pulled out onto the road to leave. I walked toward Morgan's car, where she and Jen were waiting for me. Boston PD Detective Connor was standing by our car. He motioned me aside so we could speak privately.

"Thank you for coming," I said.

"My condolences on your brother, Mackenzie. And I want to thank you for your help."

"I went to see Costa."

Connor shrugged his shoulders. "Nothing you do surprises me."

"He didn't deny knowing about Sheila's murder. He can take it to his grave."

"Do me a favor. Next time you have a case in town, please don't tell me."

"I'll be sure of that, Detective." He held out his hand and I shook it. He said goodbye this time as he turned to go back to his car. After the other mourners drifted back to their cars, I stayed behind, returning to the gravesite, with Morgan and Jen waiting for me on the road.

It began raining gently again, that misty warm precipitation common to Boston summers that brings steam up from the grass and underbrush along the water. I looked out over the lake, remembering the times Kenneth and I, as kids, found solace together from the incoming adult world. During the mild weather we were always exploring the shores of our lake in a small boat or paddling silently in our canoe up along the river that fed it. Kenneth didn't make it to that adult world. I would have to keep moving upriver for the both of us.

Printed in Great Britain
by Amazon